AESTRANGEL

THE

FALLEN

THE AESTRANGEL TRINITY

AESTRANGEL
THE
FALLEN

MARIA DEVIVO

4 Horsemen
Publications, Inc.

4 Horsemen Publications, Inc.
1497 Main St. Suite 169
Dunedin, FL 34698
4horsemenpublications.com
info@4horsemenpublications.com

Cover & Typesetting by Niki Tantillo
Edited by Laura Mita

Library of Congress Control Number: 2023934352

Paperback ISBN-13: 978-1-64450-871-8
Hardcover ISBN-13: 978-1-64450-926-5
Audiobook ISBN-13: 978-1-64450-928-9
Ebook ISBN-13: 978-1-64450-927-2

DEDICATION

For Joe—my angel and demon rolled into one. I'll wait for you in Ilarium and Asphodel for all eternity.

For Conchetta—ride or die. You are the only one who understands the struggle.

For Morgan—it's always for you and always will be for you.

TABLE OF CONTENTS

PROLOGUE

Humankind has experienced many different eras of time, and regardless of the date, the year, the socio-economic position, civil unrest, or war-time or blissful peace, one of the common core values binding most humans together is faith—faith in a god, an idea, a higher power, an ultimate judge-jury-executioner, faith in humans themselves. At the turn of the 21st century, approximately 96% of the world's population believed in a "god." It had also been over two thousand years since a man named Jesus Christ spread his teachings of peace and love worldwide. Devout followers of Christianity praised his name, worshipped him and his teachings, and believed that he was their God turned flesh. Even non-Christians knew of the man, the legend. In the end, the message of the Christian Messiah rang true for all of humankind ... peace, love, love thy neighbor, do onto others...

But on the eve of the Dark Time, a new deity rose, striking fear into the hearts of believers worldwide. For the past two thousand years—the Dark Time, Machine Time, War

Time, Cold Time, Restoration Time, Peace Time—through each new epoch of life, humans have feared the most brutal force to ever terrorize man's every plane of existence, and that fear has replaced the notions of love and peace set four millennia ago. To even speak the name of Christ is to blaspheme against the Dark One, a sin punishable by eternal damnation.

Old Spain calls her "La Estrella de la Noche," the Evening Star, as the legends of her birth include tales of how God created one angel from the purest star matter in the universe and breathed life into it, a method he did not use when he created the other angels. People of The New Republic of the U.S. call her "The Dark One," referring to her penchant for violence and all things malicious. In the world language of Esperanto, she is known as "La Malluma Stelo," the Dark Star. In Italy, she is revered as "Illuminata," the Enlightened, as a way to placate her slow, black rage. Universally, her symbol is the Morning Glory, for its petals, while poisonous, are said to bring peace and protection. People place the seeds under their pillows in order to save themselves from the nightmares that she is said to bring. Carrying the petals in one's pocket prevents depression, an ailment that she is known for exploiting, and in worship rituals the roots of the flower are soaked in oil and used to anoint ceremonial candles when prayers are offered to her.

Despite the many monikers, there is no denying her true name. She is Aestrangel—she who darkens the sky every time her expanded wings tempt someone to suicide. She was seated at the throne of the Morning Star, Lucifer, and she sang to him macabre lullabies, entertaining him with twisted poetry of the insignificant humans. It is said that she was the first and only demon in his dark domain to have shocked him with her ruthless methods and vicious ideas.

He valued her companionship and had given her the most coveted position in his demonic army. She was his General, his Mistress.

She was the one he fashioned in his image...

-PART 1-
THE TRAINING

THE LEVELS OF THE ANGELIC ORDERS

THE 1ST ORDER
Seraphim (highest)
Cherubim
Ophanim

THE 2ND ORDER
Dominions
Virtues
Powers

THE 3RD ORDER
Principalities
Archangels/Guardian Angels
Angels (lowest)

"ANGEL"

Falling from the sky
Like a bright and shooting star
Bringing salvation

LEARNING THE WAYS

They tell me I should be dreaming by now, that the images and scenarios should be well-embedded into my brand-new subconsciousness, but for me, all there has been is color. No. That's not right. When I close my brand-new eyes, all that consumes me are the shifting shades of grays and blacks, and I'm not sure if this is something I should be worried about or not. I've been in this human simulation environment for quite some time now, and I'm guessing that part of my "humanness" hasn't kicked in yet. But I've heard the others talking and describing their dreams, and I'm getting anxious for my first one. Revalia, the closest thing I have to what humans call a "best friend," has told me the fabulous tales of her dreams. She says sometimes she doesn't even want to wake up. She says the images and sounds and smells are so overpowering, so overwhelming, that when she wakes up, she desperately longs to go back to that dreamy, lazy place between the conscious and unconscious mind. I wish I knew what she was talking about.

I know my lack of dreams worries Camael. He has told me many times the human experience is multi-pronged and multi-faceted, and in order for me to complete my calling, I must be immersed in the most basic of human functions. There's no other way for me to complete my mission because there's no other way for me to be a "believable" Guardian to the human I am assigned. And if I don't complete my mission successfully, I will never move up the ranks and become a Guardian Angel. Camael is in a higher order of angels than I am—the Dominions. He's my mentor, and it's his job to prepare me for the journey that I'm about to embark upon.

Yes, I'm an angel—we all are: Camael, Revalia, the others, and me. But, my rank right now is that of angel—the lowest rung on the ladder. My goal is to move up to Guardian, and hopefully beyond. It's the natural progression for my kind, and I'm excited to serve the Creator (or God, as the humans refer to Him) and all of His glorious wonders.

There is no time—not the way humans divide time up at least. I've always existed, yet there are others and elders who were here in Ilarium before I was created, and since I've been given the ability to communicate in human language, it seems hard for me to put into words all the thoughts and feelings that I had before. Before, there was just love and peace and a willingness to serve and please, but now there is an actual lexicon, a vocabulary of tens of thousands of words, that I'm still trying to figure out how to effectively communicate and verbalize what's in my heart. Never having had a heart before, it takes some getting used to.

We angels who are preparing for our callings have been thrust into a human-like world in order to become accustomed to the actual life of a human. The Powers That Be have replicated the physical world and have created buildings and structures for us, given us languages, infused us with feelings, and given us body shapes all in preparation for our descent to Earth.

While angels are neither male nor female, I have the body of a woman now, and I will be assigned female attributes from here forward. I rather do like the contour of the female form, I always have, and perhaps my partiality towards women is what prompted the Creator to put me in a woman's body. My wings are more defined too; they are heavy on my shoulders with the feathered tips almost irritating the backs of my arms and legs. As the human notion of time becomes more ingrained into our routine, the weight of my wings becomes more and more cumbersome. Camael has said that the awareness of our wings was important so when we lose them on our descent, the shock wouldn't be so bad. I don't know; I'm still trying to understand all my teachings. Like how we're going to be given a set of human memories specific to us and our assignment, yet have all the knowledge of our angelic lives. The thought of blending the two perplexes me.

This leads me to right now. This time. This place. The unfamiliarity of it all. Camael says this is a school, and the human I am assigned to help goes to one. I know this. I've seen them, the humans. I've watched them from up high, but actually being in a school—the four white walls and chairs called desks filed in rows with children sitting at them—is quite an adjustment. I sit in the front of a single aisle. We're in alphabetical order, and I'm Aestra, so that means I'm first in the row. Revalia is a few desks behind me. I turn my head to try to catch her attention, but she's staring out the window, deep in what Camael calls a "daydream." I look at her a few seconds longer hoping my gaze can break her trance, but she's too far gone, mesmerized in her human thoughts. The one disadvantage to being in this human shape is we angels can no longer feel the thoughts and emotions of others without speaking them. If I had been free from this woman body, I would have been able to read Revalia's mind, but then again, if we weren't in these human forms, Revalia wouldn't be having such thoughts as hypnotizing daydreams...

I can't even have a subconscious dream, let alone a conscious one! The lack of a dream and my desire to have one plagues me. Perhaps I'm so concentrated on having one, that I'm actually stopping it from happening? That doesn't seem to make sense, and yet it does. I know Camael will not let me go to the human world unless I have a dream, and as if he was reading my mind (because as a Dominion, I know he still can), Camael appears in front of the classroom to begin our training for the day.

I look away from Revalia and focus my attention on my mentor, my guide: Camael. When he was in his natural form, his light shone beyond any angel I've ever seen. His aura would pulse different colors as if it was singing in its own choir. The love from his majestic light was so soothing that to think of it now makes me want to weep. He appears before us in a human shape as well, only because it is part of the training, but even a mortal shell, he can't hide his grace and beauty. His wings have absorbed most of his glowing radiance, and they shine so brightly, ever-changing their melodious colored pattern. The bright blue color of his eyes is so un-humanlike sometimes I don't even know why he bothered with a human figure in the first place. His power and brilliance must be too extreme to be contained in the flesh. My heart swells up inside of me—my devotion to him is powerful and pure.

We angels don't have families as people do. In fact, each angel is a new species, a different being made from the vision of the Creator. But I've always felt a special bond with Camael. He always looked out for me, showed me his eternal love and devotion, and has been an amazing teacher.

"And you must be ever cognizant of your surroundings, for there will be forces there sent to impede your mission..." Camael speaks, but it is the routine set of instructions reminding us of the dangers of the physical world and, quite possibly, beyond. Sometimes I wish he would use the words of our age group and speak in the cadence of an eighteen-year-old. The practice would be nice.

"And lest you forget any aspect of your mission, remember the only connection to me or Ilarium is through your Watcher. Consult with your Watcher; confide in him or her."

I know all this; we know all this. Every angel in this room is well aware of his or her calling: help the person we are assigned, help them overcome any physical or mental or emotional battles he or she may be facing, help them to defeat their own personal demons and...

"That is correct, Aestra," Camael interrupts my thoughts and sidesteps his usual oration. The room gets very still and silent. Not a mumble or mutter or flutter of a wing can be heard, and my cheeks suddenly get hot. *Is this embarrassment?*

Camael chuckles, "Yes, it is! Embarrassment is a very real, very common, human emotion. Everyone, look at Aestra!" In a flash, the entire room is in front of me, staring at me. My cheeks burn hotter, and I dip my head down slightly so I can't see their eyes. "See, everyone," Camael continues, "that is raw and tangible emotion, one that humans feel regularly. Shame, guilt, embarrassment, all can come on in that way."

"How does it feel?" a voice asks.

"Not good," I answer.

"Does it hurt?" another chimes in.

I'm so uncomfortable, I don't know how to respond. The others are all in awe of my sudden display of humanness. My head is still shifted downwards, and from the corner of my eye, I see one angel is not in front of me with the others. Revalia remains at her desk, her face turned toward the window again, lost in her thoughts...

"Alright, alright," Camael says, getting everyone's attention again. "Take your seats and leave Aestra alone, but use this as a lesson. All of you could do well with some human embarrassment, and believe me, it will happen whilst on your mission. Aestra, why do you think you had that moment?"

He's put me on the spot, and I tense up; every feather on my wings stands straight down at attention as the others' eyes boring holes into the back of my head. "You were in my mind. Reading my thoughts."

Chuckles pop up from sections of the room as Camael smiles, "Ah, yes, I'm always there, though. You know that. What prompted the feeling, though? Was it a thought, a word?"

"Demons. I was thinking of how we will be helping our humans 'battle their demons' and that's when you broke into my mind. It startled me."

"Because you weren't fully paying attention to my speech?"

I shift in my seat. "Yes. And because you answered me so quickly."

"So do you think you were on the verge of a daydream?"

I think about that for a few seconds. "It's possible."

"Good, now let's work on those nighttime ones, okay?" He winks at me like a human would, but a ray of his golden light shines brighter from the eye that is opened. A few of the angels behind me snicker a little. It's no secret about my lack of dreams, and what's to stop their derision? We all have free will, and it's common knowledge that seventeen- and eighteen-year-old children don't always have tact when it comes to the feelings of others.

Camael raises his hand for the room to settle down. "Getting back to what I was saying before. Your Watcher is a particularly crucial resource to you. Why? Thalis, answer that please."

The angel, Thalis, speaks in a loud, confident voice, "Because your Watcher is not quite angel, not quite human, and they are our link to Ilarium."

I turn my head to see her. She's standing up in the back row and smiling proudly. Her hair is cut short, like a boy's, and I wonder why The Powers That Be didn't give her a boy shape. Revalia is sitting in front of her. Her bruise-colored wings are hanging lifelessly at her sides, and she has a faraway look in her eyes. I'm now worried about her, and I desperately wish to be inside her thoughts to understand what's going on.

Thalis sits down, and Camael graciously applauds. This gives him an opening to go over the nature of the Watchers with us... again, something with which we're all familiar: Two hundred angels fell in love with mortal women and went to Earth to marry them. The rebellious angels were punished for eternity, and the children the women bore, the Nephilim, were cast out of society. But these special children loved humankind so much that they made a promise with the Creator to forever serve and protect future angels who were on their callings. These half-angel, half-human beings became the Watchers, the only immortal creatures allowed to roam the Earth in love and service to the Creator and whatever He fashions.

"Yes, Heariah?" Camael calls.

"Will Revalia be getting a new Watcher?"

All heads spin to Revalia, including my own. Interestingly enough, I had not thought of that. I guess I never asked her before because I knew how hard it was for her when her first mission failed. Revalia has been a little different since then— changed, distant, more human. She must be getting ready to go on her calling very soon, I surmise. And then it happens. A bright pink color blooms on Revalia's face. Embarrassment. But for some reason, it looks so natural on her. Is that how I looked? She nods her head, silently answering Heariah's question, and everyone faces forward to resume the lecture.

Once again, Camael is speaking, and once again I find myself half-listening and half-not. The story of the Watchers is one that always fascinated me because I know there has to be much more to the story than what has been told to us. I mean, I love humankind—the creation of man was the Creator's most intriguing invention! They are so complex and simple at the same time. They are endowed with both flesh and spirit. They are connected to each other through their blood and friendships, and they are gifted with specific individual talents separate from each other, yet alike in their capabilities and commonalities. Regardless of their differences, all humans share the same assortment of collective experiences: love, fear, hope, death. I love them because the Creator made them; they are a part of Him as I am a part of Him, and for that, I am bound to them.

But to fall in love with them? To be so enamored with their existence to actually go against the Creator is unspeakable! I don't know what it was about those mortal women that made those angels fall. Could it have been their supple bodies? I will admit I can see why a man would be attracted to the voluptuousness of the female form, or even another woman for that matter, but to drive an angel to do the unthinkable? It doesn't make sense to me.

Humans are enthralling. They do funny things and lead quirky lives. They interact so interestingly with each other; they have a different modicum of decorum for each individual encounter, yet their souls are rich and abundant with glowing light and love (whether they realize it or not). At their cores, there is purity and goodness. Watching them makes me shine ... even when they do wrong and evil. I can get swept away in their music for what seems like years. The melodies and harmonies can put me into a swoon-like trance. Maybe it was their music that tempted my brethren?

Or their poetry! Even I am taken aback by the way humans can weave words together. They can create tapestries of colorful and stunning words that hang in the cosmos like velveteen bridges between Earth and Ilarium. I can only wish that in my human form I will be bestowed the power to craft words into beautiful verse because it truly is a power—a talent, a gift, a preciousness that supersedes mediocrity. Falling in love with humans? No way! But to fall in love with the written word? Now, there's a possibility. *It almost makes me jealous to think that...*

And now, there's silence. No Camael bounding into my brain, no loud interruptions to make me blush with shame, no prompting of the others to look at me; just silence—sharp and strange. I can tell the others are uncomfortable by it. It's as if Camael, and all of Ilarium for that matter, has breathlessly stopped. I try to breathe deeply, but something prevents my lungs from feeling satisfied. A lump in my throat forms as Camael lifts his hand and waves everyone away. His eyes are trained on mine; their intensity bringing out another human emotion in me... fear.

Without a sound, the others leave the room. Camael motions for me to come forward. As I stand, the room around

me disappears. Suddenly my wings are suspended, and my human body is dangling in the darkness.

Camael floats up and locks his eyes on mine. "Jealous?" he repeats my thoughts. "What do you mean by jealous?"

CHAPTER TWO

JEALOUSY

"I can explain. Really, I can. Well, just a little. I don't know. This hurts too much to think straight, and I..."

"It will hurt much more if you don't explain to me what you meant by..." Camael's hot breath blows on my face.

"Jealous. I know. I know. Truly, honestly, I know it sounds bad. There was no other word that came to mind at that particular moment. I promise you, Camael. I promise that I didn't mean it like that. I didn't mean it the way that..."

Camael waves his hands, and I am released from whatever it was that held me in place. He shakes his head, bewildered. *I wasn't thinking. I wasn't thinking. I wasn't...* "I know you weren't thinking straight," he answers my internal dialog, "but that's what bothers me so."

"So, I was daydreaming?"

"Yes. Very much so. But it was beyond a daydream; it was beyond what your functions should be capable of at this

point in time. *Pondering*. That should happen after you reach your subject on Earth."

"Pondering," I repeat. "Ponder. To weigh carefully and thoughtfully in the mind."

Camael strokes my blonde hair away from my face and smiles. "Yes. Very good." Then his face darkens, and I feel that feeling again. Fear. I don't like it. It feels strange to me—makes me feel off balance... makes me feel sick. Suddenly, I'm afraid Camael doesn't love me anymore, and I've done something so irreparably wrong that... "Quiet, child," he says and smiles again. "There isn't anything that you could do or say that would make my love for you any less. I am proud of you for embracing the true extent of the human condition. You have advanced so much, and I know you will be a good Guardian in time. But I worry that you've grown too quickly, and I worry that you will be more inclined to succumb to the human experience all too soon."

"But I thought we were supposed to immerse ourselves in their ways, to be more genuine in our mannerisms and interactions."

"Yes, but..." He trails off. It's not really fair that he has access to all my thoughts and emotions, but to me, he's a blank canvas. "It's just that..." He's fumbling. Trying to make sense of everything and to reassure me of my goodness at the same time. "You know why I repeat the same things every day, right?"

I tilt my head to the side. "For emphasis? To make sure we know your teachings, as the humans would say, inside and out?"

"Correct. Well, partially. See, Aestra, the repetition is..."

"Multi-pronged?"

"Exactly. It serves many purposes. Of course, to emphasize the importance of your calling, of staying safe, of warding off temptations and other evils, but the repetition creates something else in you. A boredom if you will. Boredom is a feeling that is only specific to the human race. The state of being bored."

"To weary by dullness, tedious repetition."

"Yes. And this state of being bored, boredom, is something that can be used for or against people. Out of boredom, people can dream up fabulous things. People can take their humdrum scenarios and ponder the unknown, formulate theorems, imagine unbelievable feats, create poetry." He pauses and glares hard into my eyes again.

"Boredom can open the mind?"

"Precisely."

"And you think that's what happened to me? That's why I was able to think the way I did?"

Camael nods. I consciously try to shield my thoughts from him. Once I am on Earth, he will not be able to tap into my mind, but maybe if I imagine a giant wall... "No, that won't work. We need to have this discussion, Aestra. Don't try to fight it."

My cheeks flush with heat. Embarrassment, again! "Sorry," I say.

Unexpectedly, the classroom is back, and with his glowing hand, he motions for me to sit at a desk. "Jealousy. What do you know of jealousy?"

My feathers tense up as I sit at the desk. "Just the definition. How to use the word in the sentence. I can say it in hundreds of languages."

"Do you know what it feels like?"

"No."

"Because, Aestra, the one who knew what jealousy felt like was the first to fall."

He's talking about Lucifer. The Morning Star. The one that was so loved by the Creator until humankind came into existence. The Morning Star gave everything to the Creator, but he felt ignored at the dawn of the human race. Over time, he resented the Lord and grew jealous of His people. I know the story. The story of Lucifer is the example by which we live, or rather, how not to live. I couldn't do that though. I see the beauty in everything the Creator has made, and I've never once felt like I was slighted or ignored or less than perfect in His eyes. Lucifer committed the ultimate affront to the Creator and the entire angelic order.

"I promise you, Camael, that the word was just a word, used for lack of a better one. I could never do what Lucifer has done."

He shakes his head. "He was most loved by the Creator. He was called the Morning Star. When he fell, it was like lightning piercing the center of the Earth for the first time. You are Aestra. My Star. And you are most loved by me. Do you understand?" The light in his eyes brightens again, turning that preternatural shade of blue to an iridescent white. They look like two glittering diamonds inside human eye sockets.

My heart swells again. I do understand. His love for me is beyond anything I could comprehend, and he is worried about me like a father would worry about a daughter. I rise and approach him, throwing my angel-winged arms around his neck. My blonde hair falls over his shoulder, shrouding us in cascades of gold.

"Go home," he whispers. "We will meet again tomorrow."

I prefer floating to walking, but Camael says I need to get adjusted to using my legs. When he told me to go "home," he was referring to the mirage of an apartment complex The Powers That Be assembled for us fledgling Guardians. It's a place where we can all be together: socialize, work on our human traits, experience a home with a kitchen, a bedroom, and a living room—foreign objects and concepts to our ethereal presence. I really want to walk back to the complex, but I'm feeling a little dejected after my incident with Camael that my full attention is not concentrated on the motion of each leg going in front of the other. When I approach the front door, I realize I've glided the entire way to my building.

Revalia and I share a unit in the building. We each have our own bedrooms, which is nice for privacy, but every other room is shared, and that's nice too. Revalia and I have always been bonded, meaning there is a special connection between her and me. Someone once said that if angels had true families, Revalia and I would be sisters. She is a good sister... if that's what I'm to call her. Or best friend. I'm not fully sure about the technical aspects. I do know sometimes girls and women view their best friends as they would view their sisters, so I guess it's all the same. From the beginning of my existence, there has always been Revalia. I think the simile most often used is "two peas in a pod," yet we're not peas, and we certainly did not form in a pod!

I walk into the apartment and see her sitting on the couch. Her legs are tucked to her chest, and her face is resting on the tops of her knees. Her wings are completely folded behind her back, and she looks so human with an unfamiliar expression on her face. I can't define that emotion. It doesn't register with me.

I sit down beside her and reach out to touch her shoulder; she flinches when I make contact, so lost in her thoughts that she's startled to see me there. "Aestra," she says, "are you okay?"

I guess she's referring to the way Camael dismissed everyone from class. "Yes, yes, I'm fine. Just a misunderstanding, I suppose."

"Are you in major trouble with Cam, or what?"

I shake my head. "No. No. I straightened it out."

She sighs heavily with relief, "Oh, good. I was worried there for a while."

"No worries. Not about me at least. But I am worried about you." I reach out to brush a piece of her chestnut hair from her face, but she pulls away from me, like recoiling from a venomous sting. I stiffen, alarmed, but I manage to force a smile. "Where are your wings, beautiful star?"

"Oh, they're here ... resting." A small grin creeps on her cheeks, but there's a timbre to her voice that is so far away, so far gone.

I fold in my wings as well, hoping to mirror her aura, to make her feel more comfortable so she'll open up to me. My heart wants to cry because I take one look at her face and know something is not right. I realize the limitations of my human shell because I can't hear her, can't heal her, and it's driving me mad on the inside, and I don't have a vocabulary word to define what I'm feeling.

"Rage?" she whispers. "No. Helplessness."

"Huh? How did you? You can't..."

"It doesn't take a mind reader to read what's on your face! You should practice in the mirror a little bit more on how to mask your feelings." She chuckles quietly.

"Well, you're one to talk! You're certainly not hiding how you're feeling. Well, maybe you are 'cause I can't pinpoint what it is exactly, but you've been acting so strangely all day, and if I didn't have this body I would engulf you in pink light to make you smile and laugh, and..."

She lowers her legs to the floor and dips her head onto my shoulder. "You know pink is my favorite color."

"So, are you going to talk to me now? Stop making me feel this..."

"Rage? Helplessness?"

"Both!" I shout, and she begins to laugh.

She strokes my hair down my back in a loving way. "Oh, Aestra," she sighs. "I'll be going soon. It's getting close, I can tell. I felt it when I woke up this morning. It was like the last time when I had to go. Camael will be giving me my final instructions shortly, and I'll have to start the process all over again."

"So, are you sad about going? Mad? Scared? Why are you moping and acting all weird?"

She stops and stares at me for a few seconds. She's looking at me, looking through me, penetrating my core. There's a sadness in her eyes, and I think, *This isn't right, angels should never feel like this!*

"That's the problem, Aestra. I don't feel anything. No joy, no sorrow, no anticipation about my new calling. Nothing."

I'm confused. I've never felt nothing. Never had an absence of feeling. The only emotions I ever knew were joy, and happiness, and love, and devotion, but they weren't emotions, per se. It was me. It was my essence, my being, my willingness to do good, my existence. It wasn't until I was placed in this body that I had a whole other range of emotions to deal with and adjust to.

"Nothing?" I repeat.

"Nothing. Not a single feeling."

I stand up, perplexed. The weight of my retracted wings bothers me, so I quickly unfold them to alleviate some of

the pressure off my back. My feathers rustle with a loudness that fills the room; the sound echoes the clamoring thoughts rushing through my mind. I race through all my teachings with Camael—all the words and their meanings, all the languages and their origins, all the traditions and nations of the people we are to serve—and nothing registers, nothing clicks. I remember today and my discussion about shame and guilt and jealousy and...

"Boredom?" I ask as I turn on my heel.

She shakes her head and smirks. She gingerly folds her hands in her lap, and I notice her wings behind her are struggling to retract more tightly. "Cam gave you the 'boredom' speech, didn't he?"

I nod as she stands up to meet me. Her height is equal to mine, but she does not flare out her wings. Why doesn't she flare out her wings? That is our angelic greeting to each other, our sign of fellowship and good faith. Sometimes when our wings brush up against each other, it sends bolts of electricity throughout our bodies, infusing us with each other's grace. And now, she stands before me, angel to angel, and she denies me our angelic embrace?

"Revalia, I don't understand. I'm just too new at this."

"Don't worry," she says. "It's late, and I'm fine. Truly. Stop worrying about me. You have your own issues to attend to! Go to bed. Try to have that dream."

She leans over and kisses me on the cheek before retiring to her room.

CHAPTER THREE

ISHIM

Again, I wake with no clear memory of what occurred during sleep. No dream, that's for sure. I was told that when the dream happens, I would be fully aware of it and remember every last detail. All that took place last night was the same old colors and shapes. There was distant music in the background, and for a split second, I think maybe that was enough—that the music in my human subconsciousness would constitute a dream. But no. No such luck. As I stretch my arms over my head and my hearing comes into full awareness, I realize the music I hear is Revalia singing. The songs of angels are beyond human comprehension, and I am grateful that the ability to create harmonies, melodies, and full-blown symphonies from one source was not taken away when we were packaged in the flesh. Revalia's choir is glorious. I surmise she's back to herself today, which is good because it pained me to see her so ... lost.

"Dream?" she calls over her shoulder as I enter the kitchen.

I give a "thumbs down" motion of my hand, and she crinkles her nose.

"Sorry," she says as her mouth turns down, "but that was a great 'person-gesture!'"

I bow my head. "Why, thank you. Glad to see you're feeling better. Beautiful chorus."

"Thanks. Hope it didn't wake you."

"That's fine. Nothing like some splendid music to start the day." I pause for a second, studying her movements, hoping to glean a sense of her disposition, but she's cut off from me, busying herself around the kitchen with last-minute rituals before we have to head to class. I come up behind her and tap her shoulder. She spins around, almost frantically, and catches my gaze. Her wings are tucked in again.

I clasp onto her shoulders and look her dead in the eyes, "Are you feeling better?"

She smiles, but it looks rather forced, "I'm fine," she says. "Can we go, now?"

I nod my head, and we leave.

When we arrive at our meeting place, our classroom if you will, the other angels are standing around whispering hurriedly to each other. I choose to ignore them; their gossipy ways are infantile to me, too human in a way that makes me cringe. One thing I do not love about people is their tendency to hurt one another, and my brethren have sadly taken to that trait all too quickly. I know they're speculating about what transpired between Camael and me, and I know they're wondering why Revalia has been brooding as of late.

Camael appears as I hear Thalis say, "I think she was hanged in the sky." Again, referring to my "punishment" for something they are desperately trying to figure out because they are not privy to my thoughts and know not of the word

I thought. This is a good thing because, I think if they knew, it would upset them and possibly make them fearful of me. Human thoughts are best private. If I had wanted them to hear it, I would have spoken it out loud. I guess that's a benefit of being in a human shape. I guess that's why Revalia had reveled in her privacy and forced me into giving her so much attention while I pulled information out of her last night—she was being ... human.

"Ishim," he says, silencing the class. The others who are still standing scramble for their seats. "Ishim, Ishim, Ishim," he repeats as the final stragglers find their desks. "Tell me. Ishim."

I don't like sitting in front very much because it always forces me to turn my head around when someone else offers a response, but no one's responding now. No one has an answer. Oddly, no one wants to say anything. Is there a sense of fear now, or is that a general boredom that has descended upon the room? I'd raise my hand now, but I honestly don't want to talk. I bet Camael is in everyone's head right now, scanning our thoughts, sensing the reason behind the blanketed apprehension.

"Lozhure? Heariah? Anyone?" He fishes, but there's still no response. "Come on, my stars, this is an important concept, and we've gone over it many times."

Finally, Thalis speaks up. "Ishim. A human soul granted entrance into Ilarium."

"Thank you for participating, Thalis." Camael praises. "You are correct. Here is where the humans are unclear on the fate of their spirit, their souls, their breath. If the Cherubim deem a human soul worthy, they will be given the status of Ishim for the rest of time. The Ishim are angelic creatures, but they are not technically angels. They are given wings, and a certain range of power to see the physical world, to

look over their progeny, and to experience the advancements of the human condition, but they do not have the full extent of knowledge and grace as we do. As angels, we can interact with the Ishim, which of course, will be beneficial to you if you are able to reunite with your calling. And when a soul is not deemed worthy of Ilarium? What is to become of that person's breath?"

"They are re-absorbed into the breath of the Divine Creator. They cease to exist," someone behind me calls out.

"Yes. There is an expression often used in the human lexicon: Lights out. Learn that expression. Know its meaning and be able to use it in conversation, but do not reveal to them the truth behind it, for faith in their soul's immortal and divine existence after death is sometimes all a person has. And whether or not they will be blessed with that privilege is truly something that happens the moment of their earthly passing. It is not ours to take that hope from them."

I nod my head in agreement. I take what Camael says very seriously, very literally. The last thing I want is to betray my oath as a higher being, and I have pledged my love to the Creator, to Camael, and to the human race that I will do what it takes to serve them.

"And so," he continues, "as they ready themselves for their calling, they have been too focused in their teachings. I was waiting until the right time to tell you this, but Revalia and Lozhure, your first callings have been granted entrance into Ilarium. When you both return from your second mission, we will have a proper reunion for all of you."

Camael is smiling; his light shines through the entire room with a glittery brilliance. I turn to Revalia, who is not. In fact, her face darkens as the others stare in wonder. Is she in shock? Some of the others start to clap, but something inside me says that might not be the appropriate reaction at the present time. I get the sense that Revalia is not at all happy about this. Then, I glance over at Lozhure. He, too, is motionless in his seat, eyes fixed on the floor, a sense of unease darkening his aura. Camael waves his hand, and everyone stands to leave.

A quick lesson today. A harsh lesson today. Camael glances over at me and furrows his brow as if to say he heard me. I know he heard me, but I can't help thinking the truth. I can't help thinking that Revalia is somehow being tested, or punished, or...

Camael catches my eye yet again, raises a finger to his lips, silences me, silences my thoughts, and leaves. I leave too, and this time it's Revalia who stays behind.

—✕–✕–✳–✕–✕—

I sprawl out on my bed, letting my wings hang over the sides. The manufactured gravity in my environment pulls on each individual feather, making my shoulders ache from the noticed weight. I know my wings will be released from me when I embark on my journey, the final act of my temporary human transformation. The tips of my wings touch the floor as I swish them back and forth on the wood surface. Sleep will not come to me anytime soon, so I'm left here to think, to daydream, and to ponder.

Revalia.

My dear, sweet friend. I have no idea how to help her or what words to say to her to get her through this troublesome time. I thought for sure when Camael announced her first calling was now an Ishim she would have been thrilled, but again, what do I know? I wasn't there. I didn't experience what she did. I have no knowledge of the pain of her loss.

What I do know is that she tried her best, and that's all we can do, right?

Revalia's first calling was to a twelve-year-old girl who was being severely bullied by her classmates. Revalia had completed her training, was given the shape of a twelve-year-old girl, and set out on her mission to give the young one a new viewpoint on the world and to reassure her that there were good people out there. Unfortunately for Revalia, her child was far beyond reach—more so than anyone had anticipated, and she committed suicide before Revalia could complete her assignment.

I know this must have devastated Revalia to the core. A failed calling. A lost life. It was very rare, but it did happen from time to time. I guess I never understood the extent to which it affected her because when she returned, she was immediately sequestered and counseled at The Observatory, and returned to training for her second calling. She didn't talk much about the incident, and I, trying to be a loyal and understanding friend, never pushed the issue.

But maybe I should have? Maybe I should have pressed her into opening up to me. Maybe I should have poked and prodded her with questions to force her to confront her own emotions, rather than bottling them up and going about her daily life as if nothing happened, but she's good at hiding her feelings, so I never thought to...

I hear the door to the apartment open up, and voices echo down the corridor. It's Revalia and Lozhure. I recognize the deep bass notes of his voice. She's giggling at something he said, and she sounds so human that it startles me a bit. The two of them have been very close lately, and it stands to reason considering they are both heading out on calling number two. Apparently, Lozhure had a similar situation where his first calling suddenly passed away before the mission was over, but I don't know the details of his incident. The two of them have bonded over this—their almost parallel experiences drawing them closer in understanding and compassion.

That is another human characteristic entirely. Camael taught us that when humans experience similar events in their lives, it creates a sense of camaraderie among them. Tragedy, love, life, death—complete strangers striking up conversations at grocery stores, women having a sense of fellowship over the birth of children, the loss of a parent or loved one creating an air of familiarity. It is empathy that allows them to understand each other on a deeper level and to connect.

All of a sudden, I realize their voices have gone silent, so I get up from my bed and make my way into the living area. When I get there, the sight before me makes me a little uncomfortable. Lozhure is sitting on the couch with Revalia lying across his lap. His shimmering indigo wings are covering her entire body in a feathery embrace. Their cheeks are pressed against each other, and their eyes are closed. Lozhure's long brown hair is entwined with hers— I can't tell where hers begins and his ends. They are both grinning softly, and while I can't see either of their bodies, there is slight movement from underneath Lozhure's wings.

"Lia?" I call to her.

They both open their eyes and glance over at me. I've startled them, but they don't change their position.

Revalia smiles. "Hey, Aestra, I didn't know you were home."

"I was in my room, resting. I heard you guys come in and…"

"Why don't you come and sit with us?" Lozhure says. He lifts one of his wings as if to make room for me. I hesitate, uncomfortable. I'm not one to turn down an angel's embrace, but there was something different about the way they were holding each other—something that didn't feel quite right.

Revalia's eyes beam. Her pink aura is pulsating rapidly, "Yes, Aestra! You must! Come sit with us. We'll be leaving tomorrow."

Before I can answer their invitation, I tuck in my wings and take a seat on the small chair beside the couch. I place my elbows on my knees and nestle my face in my palms as I inch closer to Revalia. "Tomorrow? How do you know?"

"Camael told us after everyone left. Both of us. Lozhure and I are descending tomorrow evening." Lozhure covers Revalia in his wing again, and her eyes flutter shut. She giggles, and her body jerks slightly before she looks back into my eyes.

I'm nervous for Revalia, nervous for her next descent. I have so much I want to talk about with her and so many thoughts are going through my head, but all I can blurt out is, "Will you visit with your Ishim before you go?"

Revalia tenses, looks up at Lozhure, and shakes her head.

"You?" I ask, addressing Lozhure.

He shakes his head as well. "Aestra, the dreamless wonder," he says, and Revalia sends an elbow into his chest. His tone of voice makes me cringe; it's dripping with humanity, not the good kind. His words have a biting sting to them that makes me uneasy. "You know, Camael can't read our dreams. No one can. He knows that we have them and when we have them, but he has no idea what's going on in our transforming minds. Makes sleep-time even more private." He leans into Revalia's neck, his hair passing in front of her face, and he inhales her aura. I watch the light intensify by his lips and fill the backs of his cheeks with a ruddy glow as he sucks her into himself. Revalia exhales loudly as her eyes flutter shut once more. I hate feeling confused, but that's the only word that I can describe to what I'm feeling right now. Angels embrace and transfer their auras to each other as a sign of love, but this display of affection between them is unlike anything I've ever experienced.

"But your Ishim," I interrupt.

"What about her?" she responds.

"Wouldn't you want to see her? Speak with her? Show her your love and guidance?"

"No." Revalia's response is flat and uncaring.

No? No? My head swims. "I thought that you would want to. And since you'll be leaving so soon, I thought you would want some..."

"What?" she snaps. "Closure?"

I nod.

"You can't understand, Aestra. I failed that girl, and the only thing I feel is regret. The last thing I want is to confront her. Actually, her being in Ilarium is bad for me, and going back to Earth right now is the only good I can see. I won't have to think about her. I don't expect you to understand. Lozhure knows what I mean. It's like a part of me died or something; a part of me stopped existing when I lost her."

"So, wouldn't that be all the more reason to see her again? To make that part of you come back to life?"

"She doesn't want that part to come back to life," Lozhure interjects. "And neither do I."

This revelation sends chills throughout my body. My feathers flutter and face down from my body's tension. Revalia stands up and arches her back. "Let's go," she says.

I shake my head in bewilderment. "What? Where? What are you talking about?"

"I want you to see something. Give you a taste. Maybe then you'll understand a little bit better." She outstretches her arm, and I clasp my hand in hers.

"Where are we going? What are you going to show me?"

She looks over at Lozhure with a side smile. Her eyes flash with a brilliant pink light, but I detect a menacing sensation in the gaze.

"The Observatory," Lozhure says.

"The Observatory?" I repeat in disbelief.

CHAPTER FOUR

---※---

THE OBSERVATORY

Why I let her drag me to The Observatory, I can't figure out. This temple is off-limits to angels of our rank and stands unguarded because angels of our rank do not normally disobey laws. But here we are, disobeying away! I'm jittery and troubled and feeling all too human with this rush of anxiety surging through me. I fully expect Camael to come bursting through the doors engulfed in a fiery aura, shouting to the holy heavens above, but the way Revalia and Lozhure move casually through the halls of the temple, I realize that they've done this before, perhaps many times before, and their calm demeanor indicates to me that Camael will not be coming to admonish us.

Yes, they certainly know where they are going and what they are doing, for every turn and twist of a corridor leads to new and unlocked doors. The temple is powerful—its strong essence radiates within the walls. I clench Revalia's hand

tighter. She's defiled this sacred place one too many times, I can tell—the look on her face lets me know that she knows this place all too well.

The Observatory is the lookout point, a pinnacle of energy, a pipeline if you will. Camael and the other Dominions gather information here about the human world, and angels are disengaged and re-absorbed. It is said that there is a record of every angel, every angelic action, every angelic incident, since the creation of all. I am trespassing on higher authority territory, sacred grounds. Unless I rise to the rank of Dominion, the only times I should ever be here are on my disengagement day and the day of my return. My heart sinks. I have betrayed Camael by being here, and the guilt is beginning to cut its way through my spirit. How could I be so stupid? How could I blindly follow Revalia here? "Lia," I call out, and when she looks back at me, she smiles.

That's why I came. For her. She has been all bottled up for so long that coming here is her way of letting it all out. I'm here for her—for her to show me and share with me that which I cannot understand with my limited human knowledge.

Revalia grabs my shoulders. "Humans are such beautiful creatures, Aestra," she says.

"I know," I say. "They are the Lord's divine creation."

"Yes, but they are beautiful." She closes her eyes as she enunciates the word. "And until you see them in the flesh... smell them, make eye contact, touch them—only then will you know their true beauty. It can be very..."

"Powerful," Lozhure concludes for her.

I think I'm beginning to understand them, and it frightens me when the idea suddenly comes into my mind... have Revalia and Lozhure done what two hundred angels before them have done? Have they fallen in love with humans? To do so is a sin so egregious that I can't even begin to imagine the consequences they will face.

We come to a golden door emblazoned with the carving of a staff. It is the scepter of the Dominions, and I surmise this is a sanctified chamber. "Ready?" Lozhure asks.

Revalia nods her head and pushes lightly on the door. It slowly begins to open, and she tugs my hand. "Just breathe," she says to me. "I nearly fainted my first time, and..." But as the door opens fully, her voice is drowned out by a furious blast of air that knocks me off balance. I can barely catch my breath as Revalia pulls me into the room. The whooshing noise of the hurricane-force wind is the only sound I hear. I tilt my head to the side to try to block my eyes, but the gust is too powerful. And Revalia continues to lead me, drag me. Lozhure is already ahead of us. The gale has no effect on him.

"Just a little further," she screams.

I'm afraid I won't make it. I fear the wind will push me right back out the door.

"C'mon, Lia!" Lozhure's voice dances above the torrent.

"Al... most... there..." she yells back, struggling against the wind and my awkward body.

We take a few more steps into the room, and the whooshing and wind abruptly stop. Revalia lets go of my hand. "Look up," she instructs.

When I raise my head and fully open my eyes, I am almost blinded by the beauty of a swirling gold light emanating from the center of the circular room.

"Isn't it magnificent?" she coos, almost in a trance-like state.

"Yes," I say, awestruck. "What is it?"

"It's the energy source," Lozhure answers.

"Aestra, this is the place where we disengage," Revalia says. "You incorporate your semi-human body into the light. There you will lose your wings and make your final transformation."

I move closer to the center of the room. There is heat coming from the light, but it's more than heat. It is pure love, and peace, and joy, and hope, and forgiveness all wrapped into one. I want to touch it! I want to hold the light in my hands and splash it all over my body. I want to dip the tips of my wings into it and feel the light surging up into the very fiber of my essence. I want to...

"No!" Lozhure yells. "Don't get any closer!"

I pull back. "Does it hurt?" I ask.

"No," Revalia says.

"Of course, it does!" Lozhure snaps. "Don't lie to her."

"I'm not lying, Lo. It doesn't hurt. At least, it didn't hurt for me."

"That's not true, and you know it. Didn't Cam tell you about how the pain was necessary because life hurts? Or something like that."

"I don't know what you're talking about," she says as she turns to face me.

"Okay," he gives up, defeated. "Wait and see tomorrow. You'll remember the feeling. You'll remember."

She grabs onto my shoulders. "Don't listen to him. Don't let anything he says scare you. That's not why I brought you here. I want you to see something."

I don't know if I want to see what she has to show me. I'm scared right now—their exchange, the wind, the hypnotic light. My body is racing, wings folded inward, hands shaking. I shouldn't be here, I shouldn't be here, I shouldn't be...

Lozhure stands underneath a woven tapestry on the wall. He motions for the two of us to join him. Once again, Revalia takes my hand and walks me over to him. As I get closer, I realize it's not a tapestry but rather a giant window. Only, this window does not show the landscape of Ilarium, it shows the setting of a different place, a different time, a different world. The human world. Earth.

"This is the World Window," Lozhure explains. "From here, the Dominions get our callings. They monitor everything from here."

"We shouldn't be here," I say forcefully as I let go of Revalia's hand.

"It's okay," she says. "We're fine."

"Lia, this is not fine!" I say, my voice rising. "How do you even know about...?" Then I stop myself because I know she's been here officially before. I take a deep breath and exhale a violet aura that encircles her. She breathes it in with a smile, and I watch the purple hue suck into her lungs. It's all painfully clear to me now; on the one hand, I feel sorry about their situation, but then there's a part of me that is starting to swell with anger at what they've been doing. Revalia and Lozhure have been watching their new callings.

"When you've gone through what we've gone through... Well, we didn't see any other way," she says.

"Sure, it's an unfair advantage, I suppose," Lozhure chimes in.

"But, we didn't want to fail again," she finishes softly. "I didn't want to fail again. Do you understand that much?"

I nod my head. I can only imagine the hurt and shame upon losing a calling. I know that Revalia did everything in her power to keep that little girl safe, but her best wasn't good enough. The Creator's beings have free will, and sometimes even the intervention of an angel isn't enough to destroy the resolve of a human.

"The Window scans you in a way," Lozhure says. "When you approach it, its power reads you, and if you've been matched to your calling, that will be all that you see."

"Like spying?" I say.

Revalia huffs. "Sure. If you want to call it that. I like to think of it as watching. But it feels so good to get to know your calling before you get there. It gives me more confidence, ya know? Like, I'll be better equipped to handle her."

"It's power," I say. "A power over your calling."

They look at each other sharply, and I get the sense that they've discussed this concept of power before.

"No. Not necessarily a 'power' in the way that you mean it," Lozhure says.

"But isn't it? Isn't it a power that only the Dominions have? And if they wanted us to be able to watch our callings, don't you think that Camael would have the class held right here in this room to give everyone a taste?" My voice rises to a level that is unfamiliar to me. For the first time in my existence, a rush of pure rage consumes me. I'm infuriated at their vulgar display of power, their blatant disrespect of our superiors, their abuse of the trust bestowed upon us, their... their... flawed humanness.

Revalia flutters her wings in hopes of touching one of hers to mine. "Aestra, listen," she says, trying to calm me down. "I brought you here because I want you to see."

I breathe in heavily again. "See what?"

"Your calling. I don't want you to be left in the dark. I want you to have the upper hand, so you know what you're dealing with. So you don't have to go through the hurt and pain like I had to."

"No. No, thank you. I will meet my calling when Camael says it's time to meet."

"Please, listen to me!" her voice is pleading and almost frantic.

Suddenly, Lozhure is behind me holding onto my arms and forcing me closer to the Window. I try to fan out my wings in defense, but his body has them locked in place. He's so very strong, I can barely move, but I don't stop trying. I thrash myself from side to side, hoping to wiggle free from his grasp, but it's no use, and he's driving me closer and closer to the Window. If what they said is true, the Window will scan me and show me images of my calling—images I'm not at liberty to see yet, images I have no right to see. I'm screaming now. "No! No! No!" but he's leading me still, closer and closer to the images I have no desire to see. I shut my eyes as tightly as I can.

"Please! Please, Aestra! Be still," Revalia begs. She sounds as if she's on the verge of tears. I feel so sorry for her. At her core, she truly believes that she is doing right by me. "Just open your eyes, Aestra. Open your eyes."

Lozhure stops pushing me forward, but he doesn't release me. I'm directly in front of the Window now. I must be. The energy surrounding me is powerful. It is accompanied by a low-sounding electric hum. I'm tempted to open my eyes, but I force myself to keep them closed. A light gleams through the Window, washing my face in colorful heat. Behind my closed eyes, I can see the shadows of the yellow rays of the Creator's sun.

"It's okay," Lozhure whispers in my ear. "Just look. It's so wonderful!"

"Please let me go," I say.

"Aestra! Just look!" Revalia repeats.

The light and warmth subside, and I can hear sounds coming from the Window—people sounds, Earth sounds. Winds and rains, birds and animals, conversations and technology, and everything else—a great cacophony of my near future.

"Oh, my word!" Revalia yells. "Look! Look! Look! There he is! He's so beautiful!"

He.

My calling is a male.

I know too much. I know too much.

"I forgive you," I say to Lozhure. "I forgive both of you."
And I sincerely do. This act, this betrayal is being done to
me with the best of intentions. They are both scared and
desperate. They think they're helping me.

"Oh, no, no, no! He's gone! He's gone!" she says. Lozhure
relaxes his hold on me, and I open my eyes. *Too soon.* I catch
a glimpse of a set of mahogany brown eyes before the image
fades to black. My body collapses to the floor, the image
hauntingly burned in my mind.

CHAPTER FIVE

FALLING STARS

Revalia didn't come home from The Observatory. I figured as much. After what transpired between us, I'm not sure things will or can ever be the same in our relationship. When I said I forgave her, I really did mean it—I love her with all of my being, how could I not forgive her? But she violated me in such a profound way that my love for her is a little bit broken. It's a good thing that she's leaving tonight. Maybe the distance between us will silently repair the cracks. I can only hope.

I suspect that she stayed with Lozhure last night. I don't know how I feel about him. While we love each other unconditionally, as all angels do, he and I never bonded, and that's perfectly natural for angels to do—some are more connected than others, and no one really knows why. But now? Is the feeling that I have for him defined as contempt? Disdain? I'm probably not saying it correctly, but I certainly know how it feels. It feels hot and red. It tastes sour like old sticky milk on the roof of my mouth. I want to scrape that taste off my tongue. Scrape Lozhure out of my life. Scrape the feeling of dirtiness and ugliness he imprinted upon me. Never in my entire existence have I been forced to partake in something I did not want to do. He used his strength and power to restrain and manipulate me. He knew I was scared, and I begged him to stop—begged them to stop—but he went against my will. They both have incorporated traits of humanity that are vile and malicious. I pray they will find their way.

I know I must tell Camael about what happened, and while I feel bad about giving up Lia and Lozhure, I know I can't live with the guilt of having gone behind his back, into his sacred place, looking at his private belongings. He'll be so disappointed in me. He might even punish me. This might compromise Revalia's and Lozhure's missions; it might even compromise my own. To think that I may never get to see those coffee-colored eyes in person stabs me deeply. I didn't mean to look when I did—I just opened my eyes too soon and was able to see that image fading from my view. I know there was a face with a nose, mouth, and hair, but none of that was picked up by my vision. All I saw were his eyes: dark and mysterious. I know there are many unlocked secrets behind them, and I know that part of my mission will be to reveal them. I am intrigued by the many stories they hold. Seeing his eyes has reignited my love and devotion for the human race; seeing his eyes has reignited my desire to complete my calling successfully.

But to do that, I must dream, and that hasn't happened yet. And even if it does, after I speak with Camael, my wish of helping my charge may be dashed as well. What a predicament I've surely gotten myself into! I thought for sure I would have dreamed last night after my Observatory ordeal. My emotions were at an all-time high (low?), and Camael always said that dreams are manifestations of our emotions. But nope. No dreams for me. So, I must wait yet another night.

Apparently, a handful of angels will be disengaging tonight as Camael has canceled all training sessions. Just as well. I've been meaning to spend some time in the gardens; I think it will be good therapy to relax among the creatures of the Creator's divine design, so I head over there and sit at a cement bench in one of the courtyards. The gardens mirror many of the botanical masterpieces of Earth, and I marvel at the shear genius of it all. How humans can manipulate nature and turn it into art is yet another gift of the Lord.

God, Allah, Yahweh, Elohim, Lord, Master, Father, Mother, The Light, Jehovah—the humans have hundreds upon hundreds of terms of endearment for the One who fashioned all into existence. We in Ilarium usually refer to Him as the Creator or Lord and assign the pronouns Him, He, and His when making references. However, that is technically a misnomer as the Creator has no gender. The Creator has no body, no physical confinements. There's no man on a throne with a long white beard fingering a thunderbolt. There's no man in a red suit and cap who travels once a year on a sleigh drawn by reindeer. There's no man behind the curtain—great and powerful. There's a never-ending constant flow of life and love from the spirit Itself. The breath of life. The source of all. The rising dawn.

And as that thought enters my mind, the scene around me springs to life with the colors of dusk and dawn. The sky's color shifts in a kaleidoscope fashion from black to purple to blue to yellow to orange to pink like a child playing with the colorful scope and laughing at the wonder of the ever-changing, ever-bleeding colors. I breathe in and try to coordinate my glowing aura with the altering hues of the sky;

it's like a dance that I'm learning for the first time, and I find I can keep up pretty well with this strobe light game. But I stumble, producing the wrong color from my core, and the colors pulsate rapidly as if to say, "Gotcha!" His childlike humor is so pure and innocent that I can't help but laugh out loud. My Lord loves me! This is His way of showing me his love. His presence is so strong in the garden and deep within my essence, and His playful game is a little pat on the back to let me know everything will be okay. He has distracted me from my despondency and, for a brief moment, made me feel like me, Aestra, an angel again. I am so blessed.

The light show stops, and a peaceful orange and pink hue settles over the gardens. I close my eyes and listen to the multitude of sounds flitting throughout the vicinity. I hear crickets chirping and birds adjusting nests and the rustling of angel wings...

I'm not alone anymore. My only fear is that Camael has come to speak to me about The Observatory, and I know I'm not ready for that conversation yet. But when I open my eyes, I see Revalia standing before me.

"May I sit down next to you?" she asks.

"Sure," I answer as I shift my body to the side.

Her wings fold in as she sits next to me. "My time is soon, ya know," she says. She and I don't look at each other. Her shame radiates off her, and I know I could quell her feelings with my aura, but a part of me has no will to be kind to her right now.

"I know. You'll do a great job. I have faith in you," I reply flatly.

She grabs my hands and places them in her lap. "Let me apologize for last night. You have no idea how bad I feel." She sends waves of warmth into my palms, and I allow the energy to flow through me, washing over me.

"Lia, you don't have to. I forgive you."

"I know you do. You are my sweet, sweet Aestra." She grins and tears begin to swell in her eyes. "I love you like no other. You are the light of my life, my rising star. I aspire to be as humble, loving, and forgiving as you."

"Lia, please, you don't..."

"Wait. Let me finish. You were right about what you said about power. Going to The Observatory did make me feel powerful. It made me feel like I had a degree of control ... because, Aestra, when you get to Earth and have to live as a human, you quickly learn that there is very little that you have control over. Our power, our energy, our spirit is gone there. Do you know how many times a day I would try to will myself to fly? The shapes that we are in now is nothing compared to the real thing. When you're in that body—and I mean truly in it—you can feel the death creeping in on you." She stops and closes her eyes for a moment, reliving some human feeling.

I brush her brown hair away from her neck and caress the feathers at her shoulder tops. They are still bruise-colored; a curious shade of green, purple, and yellow mixed together. This apology has taken a lot out of her, I can tell. She looks sad and worn down. I give my wing a quick shake and my feathers touch hers. I hope the electricity of an angel embrace will help lift her spirits somewhat because I fear Revalia will fail in her next calling if she begins the mission with a defeated spirit.

Our bodies quiver at almost the exact same time when our wings make contact. She smiles at the transfer of energy but then begins to weep uncontrollably. I cease the transmission of my aura, pull back my wing, and squeeze her hand. "Lia. Lia. No. Stop. Don't do this to yourself." I speak to her as if I'm speaking to a hurt child.

"I wish you could come with me," she sobs. "I wish you could stay with me always."

I reach up and touch the place where her heart is. "But I am with you always. Here. We are bonded. Know that my love for you is stronger than ever."

She wipes the tears from her cheeks, and with her other hand, she presses mine harder against her chest.

"Always," she says, but her blue eyes are almost vacant. There's an absence in them, and I am determined to never see that same absence in my own. I can't fail...

"Always," I answer, smiling weakly.

"Will you stay in the gardens and watch me disengage?"

I suddenly feel another presence nearby and resist the urge to look over my shoulder. "Wouldn't miss it for the world," I say.

"I know you love poetry so much," she says as she rises and faces me, "so I wrote a poem for you. Remember it until we meet again, my star. It's a haiku. I think that's what it's called."

I chuckle softly. "Yes, you're right."

"Okay. Don't laugh at me. This is my first attempt."

"I won't. I can't wait to hear it."

"Here goes: Sorry for being bad. I didn't mean to hurt you, so don't be so sad." She pauses, waiting for my reaction, and while her haiku is so wrong on so many levels, I don't have the heart to tell her it's not very good.

I force my mouth to open wide with a large toothy smile, and I begin to clap. "Very good for a first time!" I exclaim. "I'm very impressed."

This makes her happy, and if the last thoughts and memories she has before she begins her calling are good ones, then that's all that matters. She leans over and kisses me on the cheek. "Goodbye, my dear," she whispers into my ear.

"Good luck," I say as I kiss her back, and with that, she flies away, the last time she'll be able to do so before she returns to Ilarium.

"It was a good thing that you didn't tell her how bad her poem was," a voice says, creeping up from behind me.

Camael.

"It was the least I could do. I didn't want her to be upset or uncomfortable when she disengages."

"Tell me," he says as he sits next to me, "what was wrong with her haiku?"

I'm agitated at the botched format of poetry. "Well, for starters, it wasn't even a haiku! The syllable structure is 5, 7, 5. Hers was 6, 7, 5. And haiku poetry is supposed to be about the natural world—plants, animals, the cosmos—not really feelings and stuff like that. And to top it off, haiku poetry doesn't rhyme!"

He laughs. "Yes, well, her intention was good, wasn't it?"

"I suppose."

"All that matters is that she tried, right? Good intentions with a far better result than last night, I would presume."

He knows.

I stiffen and slowly turn my head to look at him, but he doesn't meet my gaze. His eyes are trained on the dusky sky, staring into the distance. He cocks an eyebrow. "Look at the sky," he instructs. "They'll be falling very soon. You don't want to miss the show."

The sky darkens to a midnight blue. Millions of glittering stars emerge across the dome-like little twinkling lights, and suddenly, the first one falls. Just like that—a star falls from the sky; an angel disengages, making his or her way to the world to save the soul of a lost human being.

"Did you know," he begins, "that hundreds of humans are watching this display just as we are?"

No. I didn't know that.

"Well, they are," he responds to my thoughts. "We are the stars to them. That is their scientific rational explanation to serve those who lack faith. When an angel disengages from the source and is incorporated with the flesh, the descent, to the human eye, is like a falling star. Little do they know stars don't fall. We fall. We descend. Sure, the humans explain it away that meteorites are entering Earth's atmosphere and burning up upon arrival. Falling stars. Shooting stars. They call it different things, but it's all the same. If they had real faith, they would know that what they refer to as a falling or shooting star is actually their redemption, their salvation, an angel turned mortal to give their heavenly assistance in a limited, time-driven environment." Another one descends. It's like a flash of light streaking across the sky. Shooting across the sky. "Shooting stars," he reinforces.

"I don't like it when you do that, ya know?"

He gives a slight chuckle and turns to me. "I don't like it either, sometimes, especially when I hear things that don't make me very happy," and he raises his eyebrow again.

"The Observatory," I whisper as I hang my head low.

"Yes. That."

I breathe deeply and exhale in preparation. I haven't really planned out a speech, per se, but I know the sorrow and guilt that I feel, and I know I have to be open and honest with him. "Camael, I am so very sorry for crossing the line like that. I know I can't put the blame on Revalia and Lozhure. I know I must accept responsibility for my own actions. It was wrong to go there, and I am willing to accept any punishment you deem fit."

"Aestra, I am not going to punish you."

I pull back. No punishment?

"No. None. For all of you. Revalia and Lozhure have been to The Observatory many times. I was well aware of what they were doing, and I knew they were planning on bringing you there."

"And you didn't stop them?"

He shakes his head, his yellow aura undulating slowly around him.

"Why?" I ask.

"It's part of human nature. They were acting like typical teenagers. Rebellious. Fearless. Trying to take control of their destinies. Empowering themselves. Let's face it, Aestra, we all have free will. I felt that a better lesson for them would be to find out for themselves rather than for me to intervene and punish them. The shame and guilt Revalia felt for hurting you was far worse a punishment than anything I could have doled out."

"But they trespassed. I trespassed! On sacred ground!"

He moves his forefinger to his lips in a thoughtful gesture. "This is true. But sometimes part of the Training means that I have to take a step back and allow the essence of the flesh to work its way into the hearts of my stars. *Forgive us our trespasses...*"

Another angel disengages with a furious white light overhead like a violent light storm cutting through the sky. Lozhure.

Out of my control, my aura flashes harshly from a pale pink to a bright red, and the words leave my mouth before I have time to think them through. "How does that work when you're always in our minds?"

Camael tenses up and looks at me sharply. "Your impulses need to be checked," he scolds with a grimace.

I compose myself, steady my breathing, struggle to align my aura with his. He doesn't answer me. "I'm so sorry," I mumble, but he makes a shushing noise and points at the sky.

"Revalia," he says. "Last one."

I watch as the light zooms by. It is a deep and dazzling white light; it looks like it leaves a scar against the black sky as it blazes past us. Strong and rebellious like Camael said she was. "I worry about her. About her calling. She seems so lost."

"Don't be concerned with her," he answers. "She will be fine. I have no reservations about her mission."

"But she..."

"Has Lozhure, who will always be a competent, relatable, and empathetic companion for her," he interrupts. "You have to be concerned with your calling right now. Let Revalia take care of Revalia. There is no more you can do for her." He stands up and turns to me. "Aestra, Revalia will always be an angel. She and Lozhure can never move up to Guardian."

I tilt my head. Never move up the ranks?

"They can't. They will always have callings. Always have missions. They will forever be connected to the human world because they have been tainted too deeply with humanity. Know the difference, okay? Do your assignment, succeed in your calling, and do not break barriers or cross lines. That's all there is to it." He unfolds his wings, and in a flash, he disappears.

Tainted? What an odd choice of word to use. Tainted implies to be contaminated, soiled, spoiled, marred, damaged. So was Camael saying that Revalia was damaged by humanity? Made imperfect by the human condition? Yes, humankind is imperfect in and of itself, but I've always felt in the Creator's grand scheme of things, those imperfections were the ultimate perfection. I always thought that they were His most perfect design because of their differences and imperfections. The Creator must know how Revalia and Lozhure feel about humans; He must know of their love and passion for them. I remember when Camael said to not break barriers or cross lines, and it all makes perfect sense. He must know. Now fear is starting to creep up inside me. Will I fall under the same spell as they have? Will I fail too? Does Camael foresee my failure? Was Camael warning me of something? Is my calling destined to die?

I think of my calling—the boy with the brown eyes. Majestic eyes. Eyes that speak volumes of riddles. I exhale with a desire and determination to know those eyes, save those eyes. Trails of Revalia's disengagement dissipate in the sky. All is dark.

No, Camael, I will not fail. I will not become tainted. I will figure out the meaning behind your enigmatic words and the enigmatic soul of my calling. I can and will do this!

CHAPTER SIX

THE DESTINY OF FREEWILL

"**H**er name is Ruth Sterling. She is a case worker for the Department of Social Services. She helps children get foster care and places them in group homes when necessary. She does remarkable work and is well-respected within the community."

I'm in the final stretch of Training. No longer am I in Camael's simulated classroom, but I'm sitting in an office with Uriah, another Dominion. He's instructing me on my Watcher and the "background story" that I will embrace when I make my descent. I'm not sure why he is going over this with me now because Camael told me I would be infused with "memories" of my human life. I'm sure Uriah is wasting time with me. They don't seem to know where I belong right now; I've completed the basics of the Training and experienced the vital human emotions, and I've even rebelled against the higher-ups, for Pete's sake! But rules are rules, and until I have a dream, I'm stuck here, in limbo.

"Aestra, are you listening to me?" he says.

"I'm right here with you, Uriah," I answer.

"Good, so Ruth Sterling..."

"Aunt Ruth?"

"Your mother's sister. You're living with her now. After the accident, you had no one else to stay with. You need to finish your senior year in high school, and you felt a change of scenery would be best. Too many bad memories in California."

Pain. Suffering. They're setting me up for some challenge, alright. I smooth my hair over my shoulder and watch it drape onto the floor in front of me. It looks so beautiful. I wonder if my calling will think it is beautiful too...

Uriah snaps his fingers in my face. "Excuse me? You're thinking that because...?"

I shake my head quickly back and forth. "I... I don't know," I answer.

"Let's focus on the issue at hand here, please!" Uriah's white light changes like a kaleidoscope would—red and blue, a multi-dimensional shade that shifts languidly. It looks lovely against his human shape. He is a High Dominion who will certainly be moving up the ranks of the Order very soon. When he transforms into an Ophanim, he will become a wheel of time and destiny, making sure the balance of harmony is intact. The Wheels of Justice. The Wheels of Time. The Wheels of Fate.

"Yes, sir," I say in a low voice, but the image of my calling's eyes pops into my mind. I can't help but wonder what he's like. What does he like to do? What does he like to eat? Why is he in need of my assistance? Not every human being needs an angel. Of course, we look out for all of humankind;

Guardians are constantly sending people messages and, what they would call "signs." My work is a little more complicated than a gentle push in the right direction. I will be guiding my calling down a serious crossroads in his life, one that will have a resonating impact through time.

"That's right," Uriah says. "And your mission is an important one."

"Why so much pain?" I ask.

Uriah pulls back a bit, confused. "It's important to the mission," he replies matter-of-factly.

I don't like the sound of that very much. I've never experienced a tragedy or trauma, and the thought of being imparted with a rush of memories where the main focus will be pain and suffering is a bit overwhelming. Will I be able to mentally handle human emotion? Will I go insane at the confusion of it all?

"Don't worry about all that," he says. "I'm sure you will be fine. Ruth will be able to guide you through this. She's done it before, and she is, by far, one of the most excellent and capable Watchers we have. She will help you to cope with the newness of your body and the onslaught of memories that will invade your conscious and subconscious mind. She will make you comfortable and keep you safe. You will not have any contact with Camael or me or any of the other angels for that matter. Because she is a Watcher, the only living creature on Earth with angelic-like abilities, she will have direct contact with Camael and relay messages back to you."

"Aunt Ruth," I correct.

Uriah smiles and purple light illuminates the room. "You're catching on."

"Yes. I'm a fast learner," I say with a hint of sarcasm.

"We know," he answers, and his voice is like a thousand singing angels filling my ears. He speaks with the voice of

The Powers—scores of angels who have chosen me for this calling, and I tremble with gratefulness, tremble at the magnificence of the sound and the gravity of my assignment. I bow my head with great respect and awe, but as the image of my calling's mysterious eyes makes its way into my consciousness again, I'm suddenly unsettled. I was chosen for this mission—handpicked by The Powers That Be—*but what if I fail? Do I end up like Revalia? What if I don't want it? What if I don't want to do this?*

Uriah puts his arms lovingly around my shoulder. His force is so magnanimous his energy surges through every orifice of my human shape. Then, I realize there is something different about him. Uriah doesn't have wings. "But you will do it, Aestra," he says. "Your love is so great that you are an obedient creation of the Lord. And don't feel any shame for the thoughts you have. It is only natural to assess the value between free will and destiny."

"How can the two exist? If destiny is pre-determined, how can humans, or any of us, truly have free will?"

He lets go of my shoulder and twirls around. When he faces me again, my mouth nearly falls to the floor. There he is before me. Changed. He sheds his human shape, and I watch the transformation. It feels as if time has slowed down. Every turn of my head, every raise of my hand, is in slow motion. I'm in a fog-like state. Sparkles and glitter surround me. Uriah is the Wheel. He is showing me what he will do when he ascends to Ophanim. And he shines like the sun with giant spokes bearing a million eyes on each.

"Every one of the Creator's making has free will," he begins, his voice echoing in my head. "You can choose whichever path you wish. That is the greatest gift He has given to all of His children. But we all have a destiny that is in constant motion, constantly changing, constantly shifting, like a wheel."

The Wheel begins spinning slowly in front of me in mid-air. The light beams so brightly that I have to squint my eyes.

"At every crossroad of a person's life," he continues, "where major decisions are necessary to be made, a person's life is mapped out by hundreds of different destiny scenarios. A person has free will to do whatever they chose, but whatever road they decide, their destiny is pre-determined."

He rotates again, and I'm not so bothered by the sparkling light anymore. I take a step closer to him and examine the Wheel. There are eyes on the spokes! I take a step even closer and gaze into the eyes, trying to focus on their shape and color, but I soon realize that the eyes are like windows, and within each pupil, I can see images of humans reflected back to me. I can see their destinies! The woman takes a check for twenty-thousand dollars and cashes it in one eye. In the next eye, she's spending it on frivolous things—vacations, clothes, alcohol. In the eye next to that, she's unhappy, sad over the loss of her home. I look to the right, and in the eye directly below the woman cashing the check, she's spending it on home improvements, fixtures, and infrastructure. The eye next to that shows her selling that home and being happy, having even more money to provide for her family. So many scenarios, so many outcomes! Each individual choice is not pre-determined! The result, the consequence of each individual choice is. Millions of eyes for millions of possibilities. The destiny of free will.

The Wheel stops moving, and its light begins to die down. He's shown me enough, and I have a feeling that his power in this form is merely temporary. Uriah slowly morphs back to his human shape, but the power of the

Wheel has left its imprint on his form, and he is a brilliant hue of yellow and gold.

"You are so beautiful," I say without thinking.

He bows his head in gratitude. "I am still adjusting to the power of it all, which is why I have been granted the ability to transform temporarily."

But I am still unsettled. I fully understand the relationship between free will and destiny, but I'm having difficulty reconciling that fact with my mission, with my calling.

"He is important, Aestra," he responds. "He must go down the right path, and that is where you come in. His crossroad is one that will resonate throughout the entire fabric of humanity. His progeny is of great importance to the entire human race. His descendants will be instrumental to the lives of millions upon millions of people. It is important that you guide him to do the right thing, to stay the course, and to continue the straight path. He has many temptations in his life, and if he falls too deeply into it, it could change the course of everything."

"Wait!" I shout out before I realize I'm raising my voice to him. "You want me to mess with this guy's free will?"

Uriah's face darkens, and he's looking at me strangely like he doesn't trust me or something. "The Powers That Be have evaluated every angle, looked at the millions upon millions of scenarios. This crossroad that he is facing is so severe, so important, there's no other way but your intervention."

"Mess with his free will."

He inhales deeply, and I know he's struggling to compose himself. "Push him down the right path."

"And which path would that be?"

"School. College. His circle of friends is suggesting otherwise, a backpacking trip to Europe after graduation. But he must not go on that trip, Aestra. You must guide him to stay in school."

"That's it?" I ask in disbelief, because quite frankly, that seems easy enough.

"It's not, Aestra. And it won't be that easy. Don't trivialize the mission. That's the wrong attitude to have."

I think of Revalia and hold my tongue. What might have seemed insignificant to her may have been the reason why she failed. I'm not about to fail. *I won't fail. I won't fail. I won't...* "I'm sorry, Uriah. I meant no disrespect."

He reaches for my hands and pulls me close to him for an embrace. "I know, my dear," he whispers gently, but the voice isn't in my ear—it's in my chest, echoing on the outskirts of my aura.

—x—x—✳—x—x—

There's a sun—huge, glorious, hot. It's beating on my face, and I realize I'm staring directly at it. The rays are burning my eyes. I turn my head, and all around me are purple flowers. They are beautiful yet odd-looking. I crouch down to get a better view of their curious pattern, petals with circles that look like eyes. Eyes on The Wheel. When I touch the edge of one petal, the entire face of the flower closes in around my finger. No longer can I see the eyes. I release my hand, and the face opens again. I stare at the eyes. I stare at their color and shape. They begin to move and dance across the surface of the petals, and each individual eye is opening and shutting. And each individual eye is singing. A harmony. A melody. A lullaby. A song I've heard before.

The sun quickly darkens. No longer there. Nighttime makes a furious entrance across the sky like an angry child shutting off a light switch to the heavens. Moonless sky. Starless sky. There are no stars out tonight. They've all fallen. All two hundred of them.

But that can't be! Surely there must be more than two hundred stars in the sky. I look back at the flowers, those curious, playful flowers, but their petals are closed, wrapped around something that glitters from within the folds. I pry open the petals of one of the flowers, and a diamond-like jewel falls to the ground. There are my stars! All two hundred of them caught up in the fingers of the singing flowers.

I want to take the jewels with me, but I'm afraid that they belong to someone else, and I certainly wouldn't want to take something that didn't belong to me. So, I walk along a path. It's right here, right in front of me. It twists, and dips, and turns. I'm dancing and swaying. In the distance, the flowers start singing again, but I know they can't see me since I'm too far from their view, which is better yet because I see a lake a few yards away, and I would love to drink from it.

When I reach the lake, I kneel on the ground. The cool night air blows against my skin. I try to ruffle out my wings, but they're gone, and it seems so silly to be moving my shoulders in that roundhouse motion. The dirt beneath me is cold and damp. I look down at it and realize I'm not wearing any clothes. But I never have clothing. Why does it register with me now? I dip my hands into the edge of the lake and bring up a handful of the frigid water to my lips. I drink, but my mouth slurps up the water with loud gurgling sounds. I don't like those sounds. I must be quieter next time.

I look up. The moon has arrived in the sky, and she's casting her glimmering moonbeams onto the lake. The surface of the water looks like a blanket of those diamond-like jewels that were caught in the hands of the flowers. My stars. I need to rescue them. To swim after them. To save them from drowning. I dive into the water, surrounded by the warped reflection of the moon.

The water is cold, oh so cold. It tickles my skin, puts every tiny hair on end. I've never felt this before—the cold, the wet—but I

am enjoying the sensation of it all. There's a freedom in the water that is so soothing, so liberating! There are hundreds of tiny fish flitting at my feet, tickling my soles, almost nipping at my toes.

I raise my arms above my head, and let my body fall under the water. My ears are filled with the whooshing noise of the blood in my veins and the current of the sea. It sounds like music, like an angel's reverent song. My head sways back and forth in time with the music and I feel as if I can stay here forever in this underwater dome, but the need to breathe grips my chest and I am squiggling as fast as I can back up.

I run my arms over the shimmering water. "Oh moon!" I gush. "Thank you for bringing me my stars!" I take another deep breath and swim back down, this time to the bottom of the lake. My feet gently rest on the rocky floor, and I crouch my knees to launch myself back to the top. As I ascend, my hair falls down my back, caressing my shoulders with a wet and silky kiss.

When I open my eyes, the moon is gone again. My fallen stars have departed. Have they, too, sunk to the bottom of the lake? My attention is quickly drawn to a disturbance on the black water top, so I swim over cautiously to a shallower spot and investigate.

There's a figure in the sea with me. I sense the strong presence, but cannot see the shape or form. It makes no sound, and as I move closer, I can make out the outline of a man, naked, and waist-deep in the water. Darkness surrounds him, envelopes him. I'm afraid, yet I swim closer and closer.

He outstretches his arms to me. I freeze. I stutter. I hesitate. Then I swim a bit closer. The purple flowers are in the water now, but they are shut tight with diamonds inside. No. Stars. They wade along the top of the lake, creating ripples in the water.

When I'm close enough to stand up, I divide my hair in the middle and pull the sides up over my chest. I need to hide my nakedness.

"Don't hide, they can't see you," a voice says in my head. *It's Revalia. She's crying somewhere.*

I approach the figure. I can't make out anything about him, just that he's a man. I study the blank face for some sign of famil-iarity, and that's when I see them! The blazing brown eyes. Mysterious and gentle. My Calling!

My heart swells with happiness, and I leap into his arms. He wraps his arms around my waist and brings my body close to his chest. His skin is slippery. I wriggle on him like a snake. He stares into my eyes. That's all I see... his eyes. I get lost in them. My body is so cold, but there's a rising heat between us that I can't pinpoint what it is or where it's coming from. There's a feeling of warmth generating from our interlocked bodies. He slips his hand on the back of my neck and leans down to kiss me on the cheek. His lips are soft against my skin. Now his fingertips are all over my chest, running their course like tracing lines on a map. I quiver at the touch, shudder at the feeling of his human flesh in contact with mine.

Human flesh. My human flesh. Human.

His hands sink below my waist, and before I can protest, I wake up. Wake up.

Wake up?

I sit straight up in my bed. My wings are wrapped com-pletely around my body like a feathered cocoon, and my arms are pressed firmly against my human shape, hands grasping at the thighs. My bedroom is filled with a pulsating pink light that is almost blinding; I need to blink a few times to get adjusted to the brightness.

"What was that?" I say aloud.

"That, my friend, was a dream," I hear Revalia's voice in my mind.

"It sure was," I answer to no one. "It sure was."

CHAPTER SEVEN

DISENGAGE

I'm ready. Here in The Observatory. Surrounded by the other angels ready to disengage. Basking in the golden light of the energy source. Feeling its power and love washing over every inch of my shape.

My wings are fully extended, touching the tips of the feathers of the angel to my right and to my left, and their wings are connecting with the others in our circle. Our auras are radiating a soft baby-blue colored light; it's encircling us, extending around the circle as if we were holding hands in a choir song. There are seven of us preparing to disengage today—seven anxious and excited angels who will transform into the flesh for the good of humankind.

I had assumed that the moment I had my dream, I would be summoned by Camael to The Observatory and sent on my way; however, that didn't happen. I had started to worry that maybe Revalia was wrong; maybe Camael had been able to see and hear my dream. The panic rose within me because that dream, that wonderful yet disturbing dream, left me feeling a little ashamed and guilty. I reconciled that the human side of me had truly emerged, and I now understood what Revalia meant when she said there were nights she wanted to remain asleep, but there was still something off about it all: the flowers, the moon, the water, and the encounter with my calling. But although some time had passed, Camael never brought up the subject. It was now common knowledge that, yes, I had in fact dreamt, but it never went beyond that—no questions, no details, no shameful admissions.

And I haven't dreamt since.

Then this morning, Camael revealed to me the name of my calling, and I knew right away that today would be the day. I was right. My calling's name is Jake—Jake Parker. Now that I have a name to attach to those dark and dreamy eyes, I will be able to locate him quickly and get straight to work. I don't think I needed to know his name though—seeing his eyes would have been enough for me to recognize him in any human crowd. Ever since that night I sneaked into The Observatory with Revalia and Lozhure, the image of my calling's eyes has been imprinted in my mind. Jake's eyes.

The light of the energy source is soothing. I am drawn to it as the others are. It entrances us collectively, and I sense the rising anticipation from everyone. Camael allows us to be intoxicated by the power for a few more moments before he gives us instructions.

Camael smiles at us and walks around the circle. His wings are extended, and as he passes by each of us, he makes it a point to brush his feathers against ours. He tingles. It's our last kiss goodbye, our last angelic embrace before the descent. "Each will enter the source one at a time," he says.

"From there you will be merged with your memories, and your wings will be removed. After the process is over and you are made flesh, you will be taken to your destination. Do not fear what you see or feel. Your Watcher will be waiting for you upon arrival. The transformation is a traumatic ordeal, but once the initial shock wears off, you will find it is quite easy to accept what has happened to you. You will be human, yes, but you will retain some of your angelic grace to complete your assignment." He folds in his wings, and following his lead, we do the same, breaking the flow of energy that shone so brightly. It is time.

He walks around the circle again slowly, deliberately. My chest is throbbing in anticipation, and my head is swimming with endless thoughts. Camael catches my eye and shakes his head. He lifts a finger to his lips as if to silence me, but I can't help it! I switch my stance from one foot to the next rocking slightly back and forth. And then it happens... Camael touches an angel on the shoulder, and he hoists himself into the light. We all turn our heads to the Window and watch as Heariah blazes across the night sky.

A shooting star.

I clasp my hands tightly together. As a human, I know my palms would be slick with sweat right now, but I look down and see a silver aura emanating around them.

The second angel disengages. Thalis. She smiles as her shape descends into the light and swallows her whole. As she shoots through the sky, her comet tail is a dark indigo color and barely noticeable amidst the heavens. One the most uneventful disengagements I've ever witnessed.

The third goes, the fourth goes, the fifth goes, the six goes, and then it is just me and Camael in the sacred room standing over the holy light of the source.

"I'm a little frightened," I say.

"No, you're not," he responds as he touches my shoulder. "You're not scared at all."

He's right. I'm not afraid to do this. I can do this, but there's a feeling of foreboding that I can't seem to shake. "I'm afraid I will fail."

He closes his eyes and shakes his head. "Be not afraid." I feel like he knows something. Is he fearful for me, too? "Aestra, let my love guide you. I will keep watch over you. Stay the course. Focus on the task at hand." He tries to smile, but it's weak and not very reassuring. "Of course, I worry about you!" he replies to my inner feelings. "You are bonded to me, and I love you very much." He sweeps his hand over my cheek. There are tears in his eyes.

I grab his hand and press it closer to my cheek. "I love you, too."

Nodding to the light, he says "It's time. Go now," but his voice is enhanced by a chorus of thousands of singing angels. It's a melody that I have never heard before. They are singing my name, chanting to me, telling me it will be okay. I can't make out to whom the voices belong, and as I submerge one foot gingerly into the energy source, I have a startling revelation—it's the Creator! He has spoken to me! Not a fancy light show, not spinning colors or pretty animal noises, not an infusion of joy and love—He actually spoke to me. His words. His voice. His glorious presence urging me on!

The golden light is swirling up around me as I sink into the pool; it's encompassing my essence, and I can barely see Camael from beyond the light. I am weightless, suspended, and I'm being lifted high above the heavens and earth. I blink my eyes, and suddenly, I'm surrounded by those purple flowers from my dream. The eyes on the petals are singing to me, and I dance to the music. Camael is gone, replaced by the violet twinkling intertwined with golden flashes. I am

at peace, overwhelmed with a splendid feeling of joy and happiness.

I scarcely notice the sharp twinge in my shoulders when my body begins to rapidly fall. I must have already made my "shooting star" appearance to the world because the serenity I felt a moment ago is slowly being replaced by another sensation.

Pain.

Images begin to fire off in my mind—pictures, sounds, smells, emotions ... memories. They come at me, one by one, year by year. I try to make sense of them all, try to hold on to every fragment of the barrage of pictures, but they're coming so fast I can only decipher a few solid ones at a time...

Cold. Wet. Dark. Blinded by an artificial light and over-whelmed by an antiseptic smell. My eyes try to focus. I hear voices. I'm cold. I'm cold. I begin to cry. My mother pushes her forefinger into my palm. I squeeze tightly. She hums to me. Soothing. Safe. I stop crying. I'm an only child.

I'm two years old. I'm shaking with chills and sweating with heat all at the same time. I have an extremely high fever. My father puts me in a cold-water bath. My mother is speaking frantically to someone. She's crying. I come very close to death.

Five years old. I'm a fast learner. Kindergarten bores me. Mrs. Romeo is my teacher. I like her. She has gray hair that is held in a bun. She looks like a witch from a fairy tale book, but that makes me like her even more. I'm always the first to finish my work. Mrs. Romeo sits with me and teaches me to write complete sentences.

Seven years old. I rollerblade in the driveway by myself for the first time. I fall and scrape my elbows and knees. The stinging and burning are too much to bear. There are pieces of my shredded flesh left behind in the ridges of the concrete. My father scoops me up from the ground and sprays Solarcaine on my wounds to stop the pain. He promises he will practice with me. My best friend, Goldie, dies of leukemia.

Nine years old. I'm the only girl to play soccer on the boys' team. I like to play with Barbie dolls too. My father refurbishes an old bookshelf, and I use that as a "Barbie apartment building." My mother helps me to sew doll clothes. I write my first poem, "Angel," and win first prize in the school writing contest.

Twelve years old. I come in second place in the school spelling bee. I miss the word "mischievous." I'm devastated and cry myself to sleep that night. I quit the soccer team. I stop playing with dolls. I kiss a boy named Wayne, and he spreads nasty rumors about me to the whole school. My attention focuses on my writing. Poetry is becoming my forte. I'm a loner.

Fifteen years old. I go to my first rock concert with a group of kids I hang around with at school. The loud music blows my eardrums out for days, but I love every minute of it. Songs, to me, are poems set to music. I am excited by different types of music and the variations of lyrics and rhythms. I make the National Honor Society and start thinking about college. I would love to go to New York University, but my mother isn't too keen on me leaving California. My father says I have plenty of time for all that.

Seventeen years old. I go on a school field trip to Europe. France. Italy. Switzerland. I get to experience the lifestyles of other cultures. They have outstanding food and beautiful museums. I am inspired and write every day. I've applied to many colleges for creative writing. Midway through my senior year of high school, my father plans a family trip to Baja. The car ride is the last time I ever see my parents...

And now it comes, faster and more concrete... the images of the accident that took my parents' lives. The car tumbling over and over on the slick road. My body tossed through the front windshield, my blonde hair sailing through the air like a flaxen rope tossed onto the shore. There's so much glass, so much glass. Glass in my eyes, fragments embedded in my cheeks. Glass stinging my palms where I tried to fruitlessly cover my face. Shards gouging into my back like ancient Roman swords slicing the flesh of their victim.

My back.

Suddenly, I'm once again aware of my surroundings; that I am currently falling faster and faster to the Earth. The onslaught of memories has ceased, and one by one, my feathers break off at the quills. A plume of white races upwards and through me. There's nothing to brace my fall now, as the boney remnants of my wings are torn away from my flesh.

Flesh.

Bone.

I'm human now! I reach up to touch my arms and touch the solidity of my actual body, the soft skin, the tiny hairs on the surface, and the increasing agony from my wounded back. No, wounded isn't the word. This laceration, this gash, is unlike anything I've ever felt—in my human life or beyond. This feeling is torturous—unbearable. I scream out. I'm terrified—confused. The loss of my parents weighs heavily on my heart, and I'm having trouble discerning between the implanted recollections and my angelic existence. And I'm falling. Falling. Falling.

"Lord, help me!" I cry. "Someone! Please!"

I look below me. The world spins violently out of control; I spin out of control. Clouds and manmade structures rush up all around me. I hit the soft earth. Green around me. Trees and bushes and patches of purple flowers. I stumble. I roll.

Every inch of my body feels the nerve endings firing. Pain. Throbbing. My eyes adjust to the unfamiliar sights, yet, I know them all. I've seen a place like this before: a park. I stand up and take in the environment. My hair drapes heavily down my back, and I rotate my shoulders to make sure that my wings are in fact gone. They are, and in their place are two large chunks of raised flesh. Scars. The glass from the windshield had pierced my back. Gashed my back. Lacerated my back. Left me with dark scars, inches wide, and raised. I rehabbed. Left California. Came here, to New York, to finish high school and to stay with Aunt Ruth.

Aunt Ruth towers over me. A giantess of a woman standing nearly ten feet tall and glowing with silver light.

"You lost your wings too," I mumble. The bright light of the sun forces me to squint.

She smiles. Her face is soft with rosy cheeks. Human blood pumps its way throughout her body, yet a sparkle of angelic grace illuminates her stature. "I never had wings, Aestra," she says in a deep and gentle voice, like dripping honey. I look at her more closely. There are bees following her. They buzz in my ears, and I try to swat them away. "Relax, relax," she tries to coax as she wraps me in a warm blanket. The air is cold. I can see my breath in short white puffs with every exhale.

"The bees are everywhere," I say.

"You're going to be fine. Your body is regulating itself. Your mind is struggling for control over reality and faith. It's trying to overcome a hallucination and discern fact from fiction. Your human mind is trying to figure out the line between truth and fiction." Her voice is so soothing.

"But you're a giant!" I say.

She chuckles heartily and gazes deeply into my eyes. "Just for a few more moments, Aestra. Your angelic self can still see my true form, but once you've adjusted into the human reality, you will see me in my human shape, the glamouring that was placed upon me to mask my angel blood and unearthly appearance."

I don't want to see her human shape because, when I do, the angelic part of me will be completely shut off, and with each breath I take, I can feel death. I can feel the extent of my humanness, like the cells in my body are dividing and breaking down. I feel each one of them linger and die. It hurts. My body hurts. Not just from my little tuck and roll fall, it hurts deep down in every fiber of my mortality.

I am enjoying the silver speckles of light dancing around the soft skin of her giantess body. I had forgotten the Nephilim were of their own form and presence. She is lovely to look at, but the longer I stare at her, the more the silver aura flickers and dies away. Her oversized physique begins to melt down to normal human size. "Drink Me" reads the label on the bottle, and Alice gets small, smaller, smallest.

"Come with me," she says and outstretches her hand.

I reach for her and take a step forward. I'm a little unsteady on my human feet. The actual experience is much different than the shape we took in Ilarium.

"You'll get the hang of it," she says.

I hope so. "Can you hear my thoughts?" I ask as I stumble again.

She shakes her head. "No, Aestra. The human part of me and the human part of you does not allow our angelic natures to read each other that way."

"Oh," I reply, and I wonder—how on earth is she going to be able to help me if she has no idea what's going on inside my head? How will she be able to understand?

"Are you ready to begin?"

"Not really. I'm not sure. I don't know," I say, because really, I'm spent ... mentally and physically.

She chuckles again. It's deep and pure. She pushes her soft blonde curls from her eyes, and I realize that she looks a lot like my mother. Wait. I look like my mother. But I don't have a mother. Not really. I mean, she's dead. No. She never existed. But she did...

I put one hand to my forehead in hopes to block out the feeling of confusion that hits me.

"It's okay," she says, guiding me through the grass to a parking lot.

"It's not," I answer with great uncertainty.

She opens the passenger door of her silver Volvo for me. "It will be."

I get in, and she makes her way to the driver's side. "I hope so. I know it will be. It must be. Right?" I reply when she gets in and closes the door.

"Trust me, Aestra. I promise to take very good care of you."

"Thank you, Aunt Ruth." And with that, she starts the engine and drives away.

-PART II-
THE CALLING

THE LEVELS OF HUMANITY

THE 1ST ORDER
Enlightenment (highest)
Responsibility to Others
Love and Acceptance

The 2nd Order
Self-Esteem/Confidence
Empathy
Basic Relationships

The 3rd Order
Stability
Safety
Basic physical needs (lowest)

"AESTRANGEL"

Great angel winged arms
Pluck the dusk from my eyes
She appears to me like a daydream
White light fantasy,
Chrome rust memory,
Hidden secrets of the morning dew
Form on my brow,
I know not their meaning

CHAPTER EIGHT

THIS HUMAN FORM

The sea of unpacked boxes consumes me. I know I will have to take care of the mess soon, but I don't have the desire or will to deal with any of that now. My head is still swarming with honeybees who are buzzing around the comb that is now my conscious mind. There are so many nooks and crannies with holes so big it could stuff about a hundred of those bees safely away. Right now, as I sit here on my new bed, I'm having a very hard time connecting the two timelines of my existence.

My grandfather had made a lot of money in his lifetime, and when he passed away, his only daughters, Aunt Ruth and my mother, split the inheritance. Aunt Ruth moved here to Brooklyn, New York, where she bought this three-bedroom brownstone. My mother, on the other hand, moved out to California to pursue her dream of being an artist. That's where she met my father, and they got married and had me.

My mom was content to stay at home and raise me while my father worked in the construction industry. Aunt Ruth never married, and we visited her at least once a year. The bedroom that I now call my own was once the guest room where my parents and I stayed. I remember Mom and Dad cuddling on the bed while I played "camp-out" with my sleeping bag beside them on the floor.

Spending a lot of time in New York influenced me to choose NYU as my top college pick. I fell in love with the culture and the history of it all. Aunt Ruth would take us to the cafés in Harlem, or we would go to the city and have an early dinner in Little Italy. Shopping on Canal Street was always the highlight of Manhattan, and the museums and libraries always filled my head with wonder and awe. I couldn't get enough of the fast-paced, noise-filled, no-nonsense way of life.

Mom was not pleased at all when I told her I wanted to go to NYU. I think she was more fearful of what would happen to her if I left rather than what would happen to me in New York. My mother and I were attached at the hip, and I think the thought of me moving away devastated her. She was more than a mother to me... She was my best friend, my confidante. Even when I withdrew from the whole "circle of friends" scene, my mother was always by my side. My chest is heavy, and I try to stifle the oncoming sobs. I roll over onto my side. On the nightstand, there is a picture frame collage: pictures of my parents and me at the Empire State Building, Aunt Ruth with her arms around my mother, me and my mom holding up department store bags while shopping on 86th Street. I was only twelve years old, but I felt so grown up, like an adult walking around the city streets talking and laughing like some high-class socialite. My mother looked so happy in that picture, I guess because it was a happy time in her life—being with her "favorite girls." Aunt Ruth was her only sister, and I was her only child, her baby, her angel...

I stop myself because I realize that these are fabricated memories. No, they happened. They were and are real. My mother and father touched the lives of many people around them, but their lives were orchestrated, implanted rather, by The Powers That Be, to serve one purpose and one purpose only—for me to help my calling. I close my eyes at the enormity of this conundrum. I did all those things, experienced all those emotions, took part in all those conversations, survived that accident that took their lives, but I know I really didn't—I couldn't have... I'm an angel.

Aunt Ruth comes into the room with a mug in her hand. She's certainly a woman: average height and build, dirty blonde hair that is short and curly, attractive. Her features are strikingly similar to my mother's, but as I look at her, I see remnants of her silver aura flickering around her shoulders. Not quite angel, not quite human, the Nephilim is a race of immortal beings who walk this Earth. They vowed eons ago to be the Watchers of angels who were on missions. In her true form, she was like a goddess. There must be some strong spell hiding her true shape.

She sits at the edge of the bed and hands the cup to me. "Cocoa," she says. "Extra marshmallows. The way you like it."

"Really? That's the way I like it?" I answer although I know full well that I love my hot chocolate with a ton of mini marshmallows covering the lip of the mug.

She narrows her brow for a split second. "I understand," she says as she brushes a strand of hair from her eyes. "Still feeling a bit confused?"

I nod my head and sip the cocoa.

"It's not easy," she says. "Human life is never easy, and now, you have both advantages and disadvantages."

"How do you mean?"

"Well, you know… It's a blessing and a curse at the same time because humans don't know… they can't know. Their conscious minds couldn't handle the truth about Ilarium, the Creator, and the Order of the Angels. It's beyond their capacity of reasoning and understanding. Sure, they can have faith, but they cannot truly know. But you do. And now that you're a human, your human limitations are causing great misperceptions and jumbled confusion in your mind."

"So, what should I do?"

"I find it best if you go through all your human belongings. Look through some photo albums, sort through some clothes, read some of your old notebooks and diaries, re-familiarize yourself with yourself because this is the last stretch of your human existence. Once you finish your mission, you'll go back to Ilarium and…"

"I know. I will no longer exist on this plane." I take another sip of my drink. Yes, I do love cocoa! I especially enjoy it on chilly February mornings like today when the wind is rushing through the alleyway between the brownstones, and the sun is struggling to warm up the cold ground but that frigid wind will not let up. The warmth of the drink helps to comfort the coldness of the conversation.

"There's a note in the top dresser drawer. It's from Camael. He asked me to write down some pointers for you. Take a look at it when you get a chance."

I nod a last time and place the mug on the nightstand next to the bed.

She places her hands on the tops of my feet, a gesture my mother often did when tucking me into bed. "Rest up. Take things slow today. I have some paperwork to do, so I won't get in your way or anything. Come downstairs whenever you like, and I can fix you up some food if you're hungry, but mainly I want you to relax and stay calm. Besides, you have a big day tomorrow, and you're going to need all the prep-time you can get."

I raise an eyebrow and sit up. "Big day tomorrow? Why? What's tomorrow?"

She gets up from the bed and saunters over to the door. "Monday, of course. And it's Aestra O'Neill's first day of school!"

I roll my eyes and slump back onto the bed as she leaves the room. The one thing that I had forgotten about ... school. I guess every teenager will do anything and everything imag-inable to block that out of their memory, even the ones who have come to be an actual teenager!

Instructions from Camael are in the top drawer of my clothes dresser, and if I'm going to be successful at this mis-sion, I suppose I should start there. The note is written on yellow legal pad paper and folded three times. Aunt Ruth tucked it under a pair of white socks, but I saw it right away. "THE LEVELS OF HUMANITY" it reads. There are three "orders," the one at the very bottom says, "Basic physical needs," and the one at the very top says "Enlightenment." It's like a ladder of sorts, and I assume that "Enlightenment" is where I need to be. Basic physical needs are definitely one to be checked off because I'm standing here in a cozy shelter with warm clothes on my back and access to food. I will keep this with me as a reference, but I'm confident that I will reach the goal. I must. There's no other alternative.

These boxes are not going to unpack themselves. In my angelic state, I would have done it all with my willpower; however, in the flesh, I'm going to have to, as they say, put my back into it. It really isn't a big deal, considering I was the one who packed these boxes back in California in the first place: clothes, and clothes, and books, and more clothes. Some photo albums that I will rummage through later, personal stuff—letters, a diary, my iPod, my acceptance letter from NYU, mom's and dad's death certificates, a poem I wrote after the accident. I left a lot of physical stuff back in Cali, but on the contrary, I brought a lot of stuff with me to New York ... mental stuff and emotional stuff, and I'll have to go through them both in order to make this life work, in order to help fix what needs to be fixed, in order to preserve the destiny of the Creator's most complex design.

The woman behind the desk is portly and smells heavily of cigarette smoke. She hands me a computer print-out paper with my class schedule on it and circles the number 0202 in the right-hand corner. "That's your homeroom number and room number," she says, but this is all pretty much standard transfer student speak. I'm nervous about my first day here, but I have an assignment to complete—one that involves something much grander than room numbers and lunch times and gym locker combinations.

"Thank you," I say dismissively as I take the schedule from her desk. I glance over it quickly. "Room 202. Got it." The woman blinks her eyes at my abruptness like she's never been spoken to so curtly in her life before. I truly didn't mean to be nasty in any way, but I'm anxious... eager.

This New York high school is not much different from my old California high school. Kids click together in their cliques as expected. The cheerleader types, the sports types, and the book smart types all band together in hopes of surviving the human experience with some basic form of human contact, one of the most essential levels of humanity. My hand instinctively reaches for the front pocket of my backpack. That is where I have Camael's letter safe and at my disposal always, hidden deep within a small notebook that is used for my daily mind rants.

"Brain vomit" I call it. That's when I reflect on things that happened on a particular day either in poetic form or diary entry style. It's comforting for me to have that book with me, and now coupled with Camael's "love letter," I can do much soul searching and make sure I'm on target in my assignment.

But there is no assignment, there is no calling... yet. This entire day has gone by uneventfully. Every class I've sat through, every moment in the crowded hallways, I've seen nameless face after nameless face. I've looked into the eyes of what seems like hundreds of boys, and none bore the eyes of my calling. Most were vacant—absent of feeling, or direction, or pride, like how Revalia's eyes had turned. Cold. Hard. My calling, my Jake Parker, has vibrant eyes filled with life and wonder. There is so much depth there, so much mystery, that his eyes can inspire angels to sing the praises of humanity. His eyes can motivate women and men to write beautiful poetry!

That's exactly what I was going to do after I sat down at the hard desk in the back of the room; it was the last period of the day, Creative Writing, and I figured it was apropos to get my creative juices flowing. As I reach for my small spiral notebook with the pink holographic star design on the cover, I feel something... a presence. Students are filtering into the room, and I stop in my tracks, continue to sit patiently, and try to figure out the source of the feeling by scanning the faces of all the students who come in after me.

The teacher walks in wearing jeans and a black turtle neck, and she begins to take roll.

"Anderson," she calls.

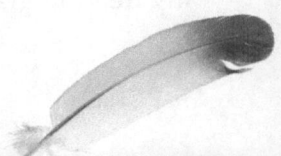

"Here," a high-pitched female voice responds. I crane my neck to see who answered.

"Bevilacqua."

"Present, Mrs. P.!" the spikey-haired boy sitting next to me shouts.

The teacher rolls her eyes. "Davis."

"Here," a female voice from the front of the room calls, and again I strain to see the face that belongs to the voice.

My chest is tight, and I struggle to breathe. I've felt anxiety before, but this is something much different. Mind racing, I rub my hands together, and they are slippery with sweat. There's definitely a powerful energy in the room. I guess I must be picking up on the aura of my calling, like a sensor or something, alerting me to his presence. But Camael never mentioned this at the Trainings, and neither Revalia nor Lozhure said anything about this type of feeling. It's odd, almost like the way I feel around Aunt Ruth... There's a shift in the air, an underlying vibration, an electric hum that only my preternatural instincts can pick up on.

"Forcas?" the teacher reads from her roll book.

There's no verbal response, just a hand from the front of the room raising high in the air.

The teacher gives a sharp nod and continues. Garcia. Hardy. Keene. Lorenzana. McKeon. More names, more "heres." She pauses when she reaches the "O" names, breathes in and says, "Lotta transfer students this marking period," before she reads out, "O'Neill."

"Here," I say, following suit with my classmates.

Before I can take notice of the dozens of eyes trained on me, the teacher calls out, "Parker" and a boy responds, "Here." My heart nearly stops. It's him! I knew it, I felt it. I turn my head to glance over my shoulder. The voice had come from behind me, and I need to confirm that this "Parker" is my "Parker."

An aisle over and about two desks behind, I see. He glances my way, and at the very second our eyes meet, I know him. His brown eyes pierce through me like they already know me as well. He's staring into my eyes—into my soul. There's a certain serenity in his gaze that makes me want to stay there forever, held captive behind his beauty. Then, there's that electricity in the air, and my chest tightens up again so that I have to look away, have to break our visual encounter. I could cry! I've found him. Now I have to find a way to save him.

I am distracted for the next thirty minutes. The teacher has said something about a group project on a literary genre, but I can't be completely sure. I know that in the state of excitement I am in, making contact with him would not be the wisest thing to do; I'll have to wait for another opportunity to approach him, or better yet, for him to approach me.

The bell rings, and the class filters out. I stay back, one of the last to leave. As Jake walks past me, there's a rush of urgency to speak to him, but I hold my composure. The electric feeling slowly deflates from the atmosphere like a balloon slowly being released from its air.

"Everything okay, Miss O'Neill?" the teacher asks as she comes toward my desk.

"Oh, fine," I answer, my head still in a daze. I look around. I'm the only student left.

"You're coming to us from Kansas, is that right?"

"No. No, California," I correct.

"Yes. California. That explains your unique name," she says as she lets out a forced chuckle.

I don't laugh back. "My parents were unique people," I say in a far-away voice.

She pauses for a moment, hesitates, and stammers, "Um, do you need help with anything?"

I shake my head and stand up. "No. I was trying to remember if I had to take the bus home or if my aunt was going to pick me up."

"First days can be rough trying to remember everything."

I don't answer her, and there's another awkward silence between us.

"Well, um," she fumbles, "if there's anything you need..."

"Thank you, ma'am," I say tersely and make my way out the door.

CHAPTER NINE

FORCAS

Lunch hour in high school is the metaphorical Devil's Playground. First of all, why they refer to it as an hour is beyond me, but I'm guessing it's probably easier to say "lunch hour" than "lunch half-hour." By the time we actually arrive in the cafeteria, get our food, find a seat, and sit down, we're lucky if we get ten minutes to scarf down whatever fare graces our trays. I never liked the so-called lunch hour. It's always been a miserable and dark place—a breeding ground for malice and derision. My human memories conjure up countless lunch hours of sitting alone, head down, ears perked to the cacophony of phoniness around me. It's only natural for humans to feel the need to be a part of something, and too often, the vacuum of lunch hour sucks their souls into something wicked and cruel.

My focus is not on the slop of food before me but rather on the faces in the room. I'm scanning, looking for Jake

Parker to show up. If he's here, I'll know it, for his majestic eyes are a dead giveaway. Last night over dinner, I told Aunt Ruth I had confirmed his presence. She seemed somewhat surprised like she hadn't thought that I would even locate him on day one. She commended me, told me to be careful, of course, and said that this was probably the fastest location of a calling she had ever seen. Aunt Ruth has been around for quite some time, so I was even impressed with myself! This further confirms for me that I was meant to do this mission, and I will not fail. If I don't see him during lunch, I know I'll definitely see him last period today. I don't know if I can wait that long.

The feeling in the room shifts, and I dart my head from side to side. It's the same feeling that overcame me yesterday when I first located Jake. Chest tightening, hands sweating, and there's a smell in the air—not the normal cafeteria fried-food smell—it's a soft, fragrant smell like fresh flowers in the morning. Jake must be close by. I whip my head to the right where the smell is coming from, and I try to avoid the embarrassment of my long hair taking a dip in my barbeque sauce.

A body manifests itself at my table, and a voice says, "What's the story, Morning Glory?"

I face forward, distracted by the person who has joined me. The feeling gets stronger now that this boy is in front of me.

I cock an eyebrow, "Excuse me?"

He sits across from me. "Sir Arthur Conan Doyle," he says pointing to the literature book next to my food tray. "You must be taking Mr. Rooney's British Lit Class."

I silently nod my head, still wary of this stranger.

"Artie knew how to do it right," he begins. "Sliced up those women nice and neat. He almost didn't get away with it, but I knew there were big plans for him, so I gave him a hand or two. I mean, really? Who would have suspected that an author could actually be Jack the Ripper!"

I swallow hard and shift uncomfortably on the bench.

"You're new here, too, right?" he continues as he rests his elbows on the table and places his chin within his folded palms.

"And you are...?" I say, my voice trailing.

"Forcas," he says, outstretching a hand for me to shake. "Malek Forcas. We have Creative Writing together."

I scarcely remember the name during roll call yesterday.

His hand is still extended, waiting for me to grip it in a sign of good faith. I hesitantly reach for his hand, and he catches mine quickly and firmly. Electricity surges up my arm and into my chest. He flashes me a wide smile—not with his mouth, but with his silver-gray eyes. I quickly pull back. My mouth drops open, and the tightening in my chest is getting more severe. Something dangles between the fingers of his left hand—a silver chain with a diamond gem attached to it. He lets it fall to the table for a brief second, and when the diamond clunks onto the laminate surface of the tabletop, a black aura flutters around him. In strobe light fashion, I see the outline of the human boy intermingled with the outline of something horrific and terrifying. Are those horns? Are those claws? I hold my breath. This can't be happening, my human side screams to my angelic essence. I shake my head swiftly to clear away the grotesque image of the boy-monster, and he quickly scoops up the pendant and sits up straight.

Camael had often told us that other-worldly forces would try to hinder our mission, and if he is what I think he is, I don't want to give away too much too soon. "My mother warned me about boys like you," I say, trying to keep the conversation light.

A light huffing sound escapes from his nose. "Yea. Your mother. And what about Ruthie? She tell you to steer clear of boys like me too, Aestra?"

There's no more hiding, or denying, or keeping any conversation civil. This boy in front of me is no more boy than I am girl. I am in the presence of my true enemy. In my angelic form, I would know exactly how to act, what to say, how to shield and defend myself, but once again, the restrictions of my human shell prompt me to react, well, like a human would.

"What do you want from me?" I say, the words sounding so stupid to my ears the second they leave my lips. I cringe with human embarrassment.

He notices and makes that huffing sound again. "I want to be your friend, that's all," he says as he sits back and moves the pendant from hand to hand.

"Really?" I scoff. "What makes you think that I would want anything to do with your pitiful soul?"

He closes his eyes and breathes in deeply. A snake-like smile slithers onto his cheeks. "Ahhh," he exhales, "that's you completely embracing your humanness. You're so good at it... a natural. Isn't it wonderful? It tastes like ... apples!"

"Get the hell away from me!" I yell at him above the din of mindless teenage chatter. Some kids from the next table look over.

He stands up. "Seriously, Aestra, I want to let you know that I'm here for you. This assignment of yours isn't going to be an easy one, and if you ever need help with anything, please don't hesitate to ask." His teeth are perfectly white, and he whips the pendant thing in the air one last time before he stuffs it into his jeans pocket. "See ya later," he says as he waves goodbye.

There's so much more that I want to say to him, but I don't, I can't... He's gone before the words have a chance to formulate in my brain. I watch him saunter elegantly down the row, like he's not really here, like he's not using feet to get around, like he doesn't care who taps into his unearthly vibe.

"The Devil is the Father of Lies," Camael had taught, "and his children aspire to be exactly like him."

This encounter brings a whole new meaning to lunch hour being the Devil's Playground. Malek Forcas has certainly presented me the invitation to play, and I have declined.

The rest of the day was pretty much a blur as the eagerness for last period ate away at me. I know that I'll have to deal with Malek at some point in time; my best strategy right now is to avoid him and concentrate on the task at hand. It might be hard to stay focused when both Jake and Malek are in the same class, but I can't let Malek distract me. I shudder when I think about his black aura radiating its ugliness around him, around the table in the cafeteria, and around me! I try to shake it off like a bad dream, like it really didn't happen, like it was some crazy dehydrated hallucination of mine.

I was right yesterday when I thought I heard something about a group project. When I get into Creative Writing class, the desks are organized in little tables of four. The instructions on the board read "Find a chair," but there's only one table left with no one else at it. I'm alone. Again. I sit down at the makeshift table and take out my notebook and pen—a single student in what's supposed to be a group project, in what appears to be a full class. A few tables over, Malek is chatting with a group of three other girls. They're giggling and leaning in as close as they can to him, hanging on to

his every word. They must not be able to resist his demonic charm. He catches my eye and gives me an acknowledging nod; strangely, I find myself nodding back. He's the only other person in this room that I have met, and even though I loathe him, the acknowledgment of another person is oddly comforting. The human need to be a part of something.

But he's not really a person.

Then again, *I'm not really a person either.*

Mrs. Polczinski starts to take roll, and all thoughts of Malek dissipate when Jake walks in the room.

"You're late," Mrs. P. admonishes.

His face reddens, and he's out of breath as if he'd been running. "Sorry," he says.

Mrs. P. looks up from her roll book and notices the effort he made to get to her class. Her tone changes as she says, "Find a seat."

Find a seat.

I look around the room and realize there aren't any other seats except for the three vacant ones at my table.

"Nice going, Parker!" a boy calls out as Jake makes his way over to me.

"Shut up, Vic!" he yells back.

"That's enough!" Mrs. P. proclaims. "Let's get started..."

Jake sits down at a chair across from me. "Hey," he says, and I freeze up. I don't know how to respond. I've thought of this moment for quite some time now—mapped out what I was going to say, how I would place my hands in my lap, how I would be conscious of blinking my eyes in a natural human way, and now, I've frozen in place. He takes out his notebook and pen. "What's all this about?"

I shrug my shoulders. "Some group thing, I think."

He rolls his eyes and slouches as if he couldn't be bothered. "Really? This is supposed to be my slider class."

My face twists. "Slider class?"

"Yeah, ya know, an easy 'A' class?"

"Yeah, I know what you mean."

"You're the new..." he says but stops mid-sentence as our eyes lock. My heart jumps wildly in my rib cage. Just like yesterday, we're entangled in a stare. The rest of the room around us seems to melt away in a gray haze, and all I see are his eyes... his magical brown eyes with the golden halo around the pupils.

"Jake Parker!" Mrs. P. yells, interrupting the flow of energy between us. "You come in late, and now you're all Chatty Cathy?"

His face flushes pink as other students snicker. "Sorry, Mrs. P.," he apologizes. But he's smiling beneath his classroom humiliation, and I'm smiling ... at him, at his most precious smile, at that jolt of electricity that passed between us and still hangs heavy in the room.

From the corner of my eye, I see Malek engaged in halfhearted whispers with his group members... his groupies, rather, but he has no interest in them as I can tell his attention is solely directed at me. His sideways glances are like pinpricks on the side of my neck. With his predatory instincts, he must have felt the wave of energy that swelled up between Jake and me; that's probably why he's watching me like a hawk, waiting to see how I'm going to interact with my calling, plotting ways of how he's going to "help" me.

Mrs. P. proceeds to go over the project instructions: pick a literary genre, research three authors in the genre, create something "spectacular" and "original" and present it to the class.

Simultaneously we both blurt, "Poetry."

Jake's eyes raise with surprise. "Okay, new girl and Chatty Cathy call poetry," Mrs. P. declares to the class.

"That okay with you?" he asks.

I laugh. "What do you think?"

"I think we're going to have a difficult time narrowing down three poets to research."

I lean forward and bite the tip of my pen. "Well, what if we did three different time periods instead and took it from there."

"Hmmm... like the evolution of poetry?"

"Exactly!" I clap my hands together.

He taps his pen on his notebook, the dark black spots look like freckles upon a stark white face. He's thinking about the project and how to go about it, but I can tell he's a little frustrated, a little distracted.

"I'm Aestra by the way," I say to break the mounting tension.

"Jake," he replies as if snapping back into reality.

"Oh," I answer, "I thought you were Cathy!"

He shakes his head. "Har, har, very funny. You know you look familiar."

"I do?" I say, puzzled.

"Yeah," he says studying my face. "Did you ever live in Brooklyn before?"

I shake my head. "No. Visited my aunt every year, but never lived here."

He's still looking me over but purposefully avoiding making eye contact. Is he avoiding the undeniable pulse between us? "Hmmm ... you ever do any modeling?"

If I was drinking something, I think I definitely would have choked.

"Modeling?" I exclaim. "No. No. No. Never."

He laughs a little and taps his pen a little harder. "Well, you could, ya know. Model."

Now my face flushes. I can't be sure ... but is he flirting with me?

"I don't know; I can't figure it out. I feel like I know you from somewhere."

It's unlikely. There's no way that Jake could have ever seen me before, unless... I think about the Window in The Observatory, the night Revalia, Lozhure, and I sneaked in, the night I saw Jake's eyes from across time and space for the first time. Could he have seen me, too? Could that have been possible?

"Well," I say, trying to divert his attention, "we have a lot of work to do on this project."

"Yeah," he says thoughtfully. "Do you want to meet up at the coffee shop between 84th and 86th before school tomorrow, ya know, to go over a plan of action of sorts?"

"Yeah," I reply, "I think that's a good idea."

"Seven o'clock?"

Even though my insides are saying, "Yes! Yes! Yes!" I scrunch my nose and pout my lower lip like girls my age do when they hear something they don't like.

"I know, I know, it's early," he says, "but it'll give us plenty of time to fine-tune some details."

"Okay," I say, sounding like I'm submitting to some grand plan that I was once against.

The bell rings. He nods, and he gets up to leave. "See ya in the morning," he says and walks out.

CHAPTER TEN

---※---

THE DINER

The annoying shriek of the alarm clock startles me from another dreamless slumber. Upon waking, I could feel my conscious mind rise up from a deep, dark place the second the noise sounded. My face is squished down into the cotton pillow, but I'm able to cock one eye open to see the time. So stupid of me 'cause I know the time. I know what time I set the alarm clock to go off ... 5:30 a.m., an ungodly hour for a teenager like me. I raise my hand to smack the snooze button. "Five more minutes," I groan into the pillow, but I know that this clock, this ancient red-faced digital dinosaur will grant me nine. Oh, the sweet glory of a four-minute gift! Thank you, Mr. Alarm Clock!

It's no use, though. I can feel those nine minutes creeping up on me already. There's no sense in trying to go back to sleep now. I mean, if I had been in some remarkable dream of sorts, I would definitely try to make my way back, but that's not even the case, so I decide not to fight it. It's 5:32 a.m., and I stretch my arms above my head, yawning simultaneously. Something in my shoulder cracks, another reminder of my mortality. I've adjusted rather quickly to the feelings and sensations of my human shape, but it's moments like a cracking shoulder that put the world into perspective a little bit. At some point, this shoulder of mine will no longer crack, these mortal bones will no longer ache, blood will cease to pump its way through these veins, and I will no longer sense the impending death of this body.

The door squeaks open, and a thin ray of light dances in from the hallway. "Aestra? You up?" Aunt Ruth says as she steps into the room.

"Bright and early," I answer, rubbing the last remnants of sleep from my eyes.

She makes her way over to my bed. Her long, pink robe swishes on the hardwood floor. She pushes back a few wild strands of her blonde hair before she sits at the foot of the bed. "I heard your alarm go off, you accidentally set it or something?"

"No, I have to get up early. I have a morning date." I chuckle, but there's no smile from Aunt Ruth. In fact, she looks at me with a worried expression. My choice of words has clearly rattled her. "Jake and I are working on some class project. We're meeting at the coffee shop to start working on it."

Her face narrows again. "I got word from Camael last night. He's worried about you. He said that yesterday there were a few moments of darkness, and he wasn't able to visualize you."

Malek.

I shift in the bed. I hadn't told Aunt Ruth about Malek Forcas at dinner yesterday, and now with Camael's concerns,

I feel as if I've hidden something from her. I really didn't mean to keep it a secret; I guess it slipped my mind.

"At school, there's this guy, but he's not really a guy, do you know what I mean?" I say.

She breathes in deeply through her nose and exhales with a nasally sound. "Yes, I know."

"He knows who I am, knows my assignment. He's watching me, like keeping tabs on me. Does that make sense?"

"Perfect sense. Has he spoken to you?"

"He told me he wanted to help me and…"

"Aestra!" she interrupts.

"I know, I know…"

"Don't listen to a thing he says! Stay as far from him as possible! He's a…"

"Child of Lies. Yes, I know," I say, trying to calm her down.

"There are always chances of outside threats, but this one…"

"I will be careful, I promise."

She gets up and walks around the side of my bed. "You don't have to complete this mission in such a hurry," she says as she kisses the crown of my head.

"I know," I say, and she leaves. I start to get ready, her words echoing in my mind.

-x-x-✳x-x-

I make it to the café at 6:48 a.m. Wherever I go, I've always been the type to arrive early because it helps me to relax a little and mentally process whatever it is I'm about to do. Sometimes I'll scribble a poem or two on a napkin or the sidebar of a newspaper. Sometimes I'll sit and think about my role and purpose in life—the grander scale topics.

A skinny waitress seats me at a booth by the window when I tell her I'm waiting for someone to join me. After she takes my drink order (large coffee, cream, four sugars) I survey the room. The place is packed with the early morning breakfast crew. I recognize a lot of faces from school and realize this must be the "go-to" place to hang out before classes begin. From the corner of my eye, I spot someone waving at me, and I immediately know who it is. Malek is at a table a few rows away. He's with the same group of girls from class, and it appears that nothing has changed from yesterday. The three of them are practically drooling into their breakfast plates, hypnotized by his very presence.

I hate to admit it, but he is attractive. He's the quintessential "tall, dark, and handsome American dream," and the way he talks is so intelligent and smooth. He must have had to overly compensate for his original form, for his demon-self was one of the most hideous images I've seen in my entire eighteen years. Human years. Quite possibly my entire existence.

My daydreaming has prevented me from noticing him move. He scares me half to death when he slides onto the bench across from me.

"Sleep well last night?" he smirks.

My hand rises to my chest, and I gasp.

"Sorry, sorry! I didn't mean to startle you." An overwhelming scent of flowers accompanies him—the smell of waxy orange blossoms sweating in the sun. *Morning glories.* "Have you given any thought to what I said yesterday?"

"Yes," I say, and I squint my eyes for a second. His diamond pendant necklace catches the morning light from the window and blinds me. "Your services won't be needed."

He puts on a fake frown. "C'mon, now. Don't be so quick to jump to conclusions. We're both new here. New school, new city, new callings… I think there's a lot that we can learn from one another." He touches my hand and looks deeply into my eyes. There, I see a storm … not a metaphorical one, but an actual storm! The gray clouds race across the horizons of his irises as violent lightning charges to the centers of his pupils. I rapidly blink and pull my hand away to make the tempest stop.

Jake appears behind Malek as the waitress brings me my coffee. He's carrying a couple of books that read "Poetry" and "Poetic Strategies" on their spines. He looks down at Malek, puzzled, before smiling at me and saying, "Hey."

"Hey," I answer nervously. A wave of uneasiness invades my being.

"You ready?" he asks.

"Yes, yes," I say nodding my head, nodding Malek away. Malek catches on and gets up.

"See you later," Malek says to me before leaving. He never even acknowledged Jake's presence.

"You know that guy?" Jake asks as he sits in Malek's place.

"Just from Creative Writing class," I say.

"Oh, that's where I know his from. He's a newbie too, right?"

"Something like that," I say as I turn my head in Malek's direction. The group of girls he was with seems to be pleased that he's returned to them, but it's obvious he's paying them no mind. His attention—his wild, stormy gaze—is trained on me.

"I guess it's nice not being the only new kid in class. You two are helping each other out?"

I nod. I lie. I'm not helping Malek with anything, and he's certainly not helping me. Suddenly, I'm overcome with the feeling that Malek isn't just trying to interfere with my mission…

"So," Jake continues, "I found these books in my step-mother's bookcase. Not sure if they can help us or not, but I figure it can help us start." He hands me the "Poetic Strategies" book, and I begin thumbing through the yellowed pages. He must not like the expression on my face because he wrinkles his nose. "No good?"

"Eh," I blurt. "I don't think this is what we are looking for." I reach for the other book, and it nearly topples out of my hands. A few pieces of notebook paper float into my lap, and I investigate with great curiosity. "What's this?" I say as I open one of them up and begin to read aloud. "'Life's Parody. A simple tragedy, encased in the moments of a dark storm...'"

He lunges over the table and snatches the papers out of my hands. For a split second, his fingers sweep across the top of my hand and my body quivers from his magnetic pulse. Our eyes lock. I know he felt it too because he gives me a strange look, one that says, "What the..."

I blink my eyes to break our stare. "Oh," I say, confused. "I'm sorry."

"No worries," he says. "Just something that I don't want read out loud."

"You wrote that?"

"Yeah. A long, long time ago. That's why it sucks so bad, but I didn't really know much back then." His face darkens, and I can see him slipping into deep thought.

"Well, you didn't give me a chance to determine whether it sucked or not," I say trying to lighten the mood.

"Trust me. It sucks. I was like twelve years old when I wrote it."

"It didn't seem so bad for a twelve-year-old. Kinda cool that you still have something from when you were that young. I still have a lot of my poems from when I was a kid."

He looks down at the papers, quickly reads the words, folds the pages up in the middle, and puts them in his jacket pocket. "I gave it to my stepmother when she and my dad got married. She and I had a rocky start and all, and it was supposed to be an 'I accept you as my mother' kind of gesture."

"Oh," I sigh, "that's very nice."

"Nah. I hate that bitch. She's nothing but a money-hungry whore. My mother was barely dead a year before that one came in and convinced my dad to marry her."

The ugliness of his words alarms me, and I stiffen up a little, but I remember that the only way I'm going to succeed, the only way I'm going to get him to go down whatever path he needs to go down, is by knowing him, understanding him, and empathizing with him. And this is the perfect opportunity to make that connection with my calling. Empathy ... the second key component in the Levels of Humanity. My parents are dead, and they're not six years dead like Jake's mother; they're two months dead. The freshness of my wounds should resonate with the twelve-year-old boy inside of him.

I sip my coffee as the waitress dances over to take our orders. Jake orders coffee as well and a plate of extra crispy bacon while I order a blueberry muffin with grape jelly. He makes a weird face after I order and looks back down at one of the poetry books. Blueberry muffins with grape jelly ... the way my father ate them. I allow the memory of my father to fill my conscious mind. The pain of losing him, the strong and confident man that he was, swells inside me, rising to the lids of my eyes. I frantically wipe a large teardrop before it falls down my cheek. I don't think Jake noticed.

"You're lucky that you at least still have your father," I say. The words are crackled like a telephone connection breaking up. The sound brings Jake's attention back to my face with a puzzled look. I take in the features of his face—his high cheekbones, the perfect symmetry of his mouth to nose to eyes... his eyes... of course, he has those honey-brown eyes that make me feel sticky inside. "There was a car accident about two months ago," I say softly, breaking my adoring stare. "My parents were taking me to Baja for vacation. The Jeep flipped over, and I was ejected. My parents didn't make it." I stop, and for a second, I tell myself that it really didn't happen because none of this before I came to be in this body actually happened.

"Oh," he says in shock. "I didn't know."

Of course, he didn't know. How could he have known? I realize that's what humans say when they're in disbelief or in awe of something. "I didn't know" becomes a stock response for tragedy and human-to-human interactions. "I didn't know" indicates to me that I was successful in creating a compassionate connection because it means he wants to say something in a meaningful response, but he doesn't know how. My tragedy trumps his tragedy, and he's probably feeling a little bit better about the parent he has left and the shrew of a stepmother who probably ultimately cares about him under the surface.

"Are you okay?" he asks, struggling with the words.

"I have my bad days and my good days," I say, lying again because technically this is the third day that I've endured in this shell.

"Were you hurt?" he asks. A natural, human response. Humans are always so drawn to chaos and the aftermath. It's a combination of violence and curiosity that propels them to stop and stare at a train wreck or watch continuous images of death and destruction on the news channels.

"I needed surgery on my back to repair the damaged muscles. I was basically impaled on glass from the broken window," I say, nonchalantly.

He winces, an uncontrollable reaction. "Are your scars bad?"

I nod.

He stares at me for a few moments like he's trying to picture the accident... like he's trying to make sense of what happened to me... like he's trying to re-create that common bond that he and I now share. I'm an orphan; he's motherless—children without parents who have experienced the same feeling of helplessness and loss. There's a pained expression on his face, but there's also a certain warmth in his honey-brown eyes that is enveloping me. "Well, you're really lucky to be alive."

"I know. I thank God every day," which is not a lie because I do give thanks to the Creator for my existence, for the wonderful privilege of life He has bestowed upon me, and for the wonderful opportunity I have been afforded to make a positive change in His most precious creation. I am honored to have been chosen to help this beautiful boy before me.

"So where are you from, originally?" he asks.

"California."

"Then, why did you come to Brooklyn?"

"My mother's sister. She's the only real family I have left, and I figured it would be so much easier if I came to stay with her now. It took me away from a lot of painful memories, and it will make it easier next year when I go to NYU..."

"Wait!" he interrupts, his eyes lighting up. "You're going to NYU in the fall?"

"Yeah, I got accepted right before the accident."

He shakes his head in disbelief. "Me too!" he says, and like a bright light exploding in my brain, things start to make sense to me now. NYU must be a key to my mission. "I mean, I got accepted there, too."

"Dude, you know NYU can wait a year ... or two!" a voice bellows. Jake turns his head to greet the tall, muscular boy who has walked over to our table. "You know, if they'll take you now, they'll take you in the future," the boy says as he slaps a thick hand on Jake's back.

A girl scurries passed the muscle man and sits on the bench, her short blonde hair bouncing like some shampoo commercial. She throws her arms around Jake and kisses him lovingly on the cheek. A stabbing feeling grips my chest.

The boy nods his head indicating for me to move over. "Mind?" he says, and I scoot closer to the window.

"What, are you actually doing work here?" he says to Jake.

Jake laughs, and the girl showers his face with more pecks. "Aestra," he says, "this is Vic. He's in our Creative Writing class. And this is my girlfriend, Summer."

Girlfriend.

The word makes something deep inside me cringe, something that I can't control. I nod my head forward and smile. Vic doesn't acknowledge me, and Summer casually waves her hand. "Hi," I say softly.

Summer runs her fingers through Jake's hair. "So, whatcha working on?"

"That stupid project?" Vic roars. "Why the hell are you even bothering with that? That class isn't gonna matter when we're touring Europe this summer."

Summer leans her head on Jake's shoulder, "Yeah, babe. The Eiffel Tower doesn't care that you only got a 'B' in Creative Writing."

Jake smiles. "Yeah, yeah, yeah... we'll see about that one," he laughs, but I notice he shifts his body to the right, causing Summer's head to slide off his shoulder. He looks at me, but

I can't read the expression on his face. He looks conflicted, confused.

It's okay, I'll help you.

I sit quietly until the waitress brings us our food. When the oversized plate of bacon is set in front of Jake, Vic and Summer both greedily snatch a piece. "You know how I like it, babe. Extra crispy!" Summer says with her mouth full.

Vic throws a white sugar packet at her and looks over at my dish in disgust. "What the hell is that?" he asks.

"A blueberry muffin..." I answer. My voice trails because I don't quite understand the nature of his question.

He sticks out his tongue like children do when they eat something they don't like. "With jelly?" he says. "Who the hell eats a blueberry muffin with jelly?"

My father did, I want so very badly to say, but I don't. I ignore the meathead next to me and take a slow, deliberate bite out of the muffin. Jake glances up at Vic, and I definitely can read the expression on his face... embarrassment. He makes quick eye contact with me and returns his attention to his plate of burnt meat.

I'm a fourth wheel in this diner booth. I don't belong here with them. I don't fit in. The conversation continues among the three, and I sit in silence, gazing out the large window. Malek walks by and taps his wrist as if he's tapping a watch. I know, I know, it's time to get going to school, but I'm sandwiched here between a glass window and one of the rudest human beings I've ever met. Malek waves "goodbye," and before I can roll my eyes at him, his diamond pendant catches a sun's ray and causes me to blink with temporary blindness.

CHAPTER ELEVEN

THE PARTY

When I was a kid, I used to like to pretend that I was a mermaid. I would swim in my parents' pool and let my long blonde hair dance wildly around me. It was as if I could stay under the water for hours. My friend Yasmine would watch me go under and count each second that passed. What only lasted a minute or so would feel like a lifetime. In those precious seconds, those precious moments of weightlessness and serenity, I would create my own magical world where I was one with nature and energy. I know now that those fabricated memories were my angelic-self tapping into something higher, reaching above and beyond the normal capabilities of the human mind, but as these days pass, the human part of me is taking over more and more. Like, it's controlling me, driving me, and to my human mind, my angelic-self is becoming the fantasy, the sixty seconds under water.

I'm trying to recreate that feeling now—lying in the bath, my hair dancing around my shoulders. The tub is no substitute for a full-size pool; my legs hang over the side, and the water barely covers my face, but it'll do. The water fills my ears with a whooshing sound. The sound of breathing from my nose blocks out any other sounds from the world around me, and I imagine that this is what a strong and powerful dragon must sound like as it inhales its every breath. A dragon—green and scaly with diamond-encrusted wings. He can float above mountaintops and breathe fire at will. My hands reach over the surface of my naked body to be sure that there aren't any scales, that there aren't any wings creeping from behind my shoulder blades. No. No such luck. And I remember there once were wings there—luminescent and awe-inspiring. My wings were a vision of beauty and grace. They will return to me one day soon.

Progress with Jake is coming along, slowly but surely, although I'm starting to look at him as more of a friend and less of a "mission." He and I have been spending many mornings at the café working on our poetry project. I must say, it's actually pretty good! We've chosen three decades: the 1950's, 1960's, and 1970's, and we've outlined the way poetry changed dramatically over that thirty-year time span. At the end of the presentation, we plan on presenting a current-day poem or two and leaving off with a cliffhanger of sorts. Jake thinks it will spark the class's interest in the genre if they see how the art of poetry is something that is constant but ever-changing. I said I would go along with the concept, but unfortunately, I suspect it will go over the heads of our peers.

He's working on a slick PowerPoint presentation because apparently he's not only literature savvy, but he's technologically advanced as well. It doesn't surprise me in the least because he's so completely well-rounded... smart, charming, handsome... but he's so conflicted, at odds with what he wants to do and what he has to do. He's told me on several occasions that he does want to go to school in the fall but that the thought of traveling with his friends is very tempting. It seems so trivial to me. Like, why am I even here, an angel on Earth, trying to guide a teenage boy to go to college? Aestra wants to go to Europe too! Wants to climb the Eifel Tower and eat an authentic Italian meal. My human side wants to say, "Go! Explore! Vic is right. College can wait!" But my own conflict is within my heavenly grace that cautions otherwise. "Go to school. There's something there that can't wait." I don't know what that something quite is, and I know there is some larger force at play here, but mine is not to question why.

I barely get out of the bath when the phone rings downstairs. Aunt Ruth screams up the steps for me to pick up the extension, and by the excited tone of her voice, I have a feeling it's Jake. I throw on a robe, race to my bedroom, and pick up the old-fashioned rotary.

"Hello?" I say.

"Aestra? It's Jake."

Aunt Ruth clicks off on her end, I bet satisfied to hear who it was.

"Hey," I say. "What's up?"

"Nothing. What are you doing right now?"

I'm not about to tell him that I'm standing in my room, half naked and dripping wet, so I make something up. "Oh, just going through some old boxes. Unpacking the last of my things. Reading some old poems." The lie drips from my tongue.

"Stuff you wrote? Read me something. Maybe we could use one for the project."

"No way! Until you show one of yours, you are never getting your hands on one of mine."

He snickers, "Oh, really?"

I palm my forehead with my free hand. "Can you get your mind out of the gutter?"

He snickers again and changes the subject. "Vic's having a party tonight. His parents are out of town for the weekend, so he invited some people over." I suspect he's inviting me to go, but I can't be sure.

"Oh?"

"Yeah, and when I say he invited some people over, I really mean he invited the whole school ... literally! And, well... you're part of the school, so I was passing along the invite."

Vic irritates me. There's something about him that rubs me the wrong way. It could be his oversized shoulders (I don't think any normal eighteen-year-old boy should have shoulders that massive) or his snarky attitude. I think that sometimes I'd rather converse with my sworn enemy, Malek, than endure the meathead's mindless blather. At least with Malek, I could have a somewhat intelligent (albeit deceptive and lie-filled) conversation! When Jake and I meet up at the cafe in the mornings, Vic and Summer always show up about fifteen minutes before we have to leave for school. And of course, since Summer is Jake's girlfriend, I always get stuck, crammed in the booth right next to Vic. Summer is a nice girl, bearable. I know for a fact that she isn't the girl that Jake is going to end up with, so I can tolerate her for the most part. But she irritates me too when she throws her arms around Jake and says things like, "Oh, babe! I can't wait to see you tonight!" in her high-pitched baby voice, and I... I stop myself. I stop my thoughts. I pull back and realize that there's a sprout of jealousy blooming in my heart, and I can't allow it to grow.

"I don't know," I hesitate.

"Come on," he urges. "We won't talk shop at all. We'll go, listen to some music, watch our friends make fools of themselves, and hang out."

I'm not really up for a party tonight, but there's a part of me that really wants to see Jake—even if Summer and Vic will be around. But I say, "I don't have a ride," secretly wanting him to press me into going.

"Not a problem. Summer and I will pick you up. Around seven. You're coming. End of discussion."

I smile. "Fine, fine. I'll see you later."

"Later."

My nerves start to get the best of me as I thumb through hanger after hanger in my closet. I told Aunt Ruth, and even she said I should go in order to further my connection with Jake and with others since I haven't connected much with the kids at school. The black turtleneck and gray fur vest call my name. I pair them with tight blue jeans and a pair of knee-high black leather boots. My hair is still wet, so I pull it back into a tight bun at the center of my head. I can hear my mother screaming at me that "You'll catch pneumonia for leaving the house with a wet head." Sorry, Mom. I put on a little bit of makeup and wait in the foyer for Jake and Summer to pick me up.

When the horn beeps letting me know they're here, I yell upstairs to Aunt Ruth to tell her I'm leaving, and I head out the door. Summer drives a red Range Rover; Jake is in the front passenger seat, and I hop in the back.

"That's a cute vest," Summer says as I slam the door.

"Thanks," I say.

"So, you know, Jake, I plan on getting totally trashed tonight and..."

"I know, I know," he says, defeated. "I'm DD."

"DD?" I ask.

"Designated driver?" Summer answers.

"Oh, oh, gotcha," I say, feeling very much like an idiot.

Jake pulls his sun visor down to look in the mirror, only he doesn't look at himself; he tilts it so that he can see me in the backseat. Only his eyes are visible to me, but that's all I need to see of...

"Hey," he says, and I can tell he's smiling by the way his eyes flash.

"Hey," I answer, giving a smile of my own.

"You plan on getting trashed tonight, too?" he asks. I laugh and shake my head.

"Oh, no, no, no!" I say.

Summer pouts out her lip sarcastically, "Aw, you are too good for some drinking, Aestra?" Even the way she says my name sounds sarcastic.

"No, it's not that. I just... I don't know... not one for drinking, I guess."

"Good," Jake says to me, "at least I'll only have to worry about carting one sloppy drunk ass home!"

Summer takes her right hand off the steering wheel and playfully punches Jake in the arm. Her shimmery makeup accents her high cheekbones as it glimmers against the street lights. She is very pretty, and I understand why Jake is attracted to her. She must have put some glittery stuff in her hair too because she seems to glint all over as if she were sparkled with fairy dust, and... the Range Rover jerks a little to the side, and I instinctively grip the door handle of the side panel. I think I must have gasped because Jake's eyebrows crease, and he gives me a look that says, "Are you okay?"

"I'm fine," I mouth to him, and his face relaxes.

Summer puts both hands back on the wheel and rights the car. "Of course," she says, "Aestra's gotta stay sober so she can pick up a hottie."

Pick up a hottie? I don't even think the Valley Girls in California use phrases like these! I catch Jake's gaze again. "I don't know about that one either," I say.

"Come on," she continues, "you've been here like a month now, right?"

"Something like that."

"And there isn't one guy you can think of that you would like to go out with?"

"I'm not really thinking about dating, or hooking up, or whatever it is you call it."

She looks at me in the rearview and makes a face. I was right; her lids are covered in silver shimmer shadow and outlined in black liner making her look like a disco doll.

"And no, I don't like girls if that was your next question," I blurt out. Jake laughs out loud.

"What about that guy from the café?" she continues to press.

"What guy?" Jake interjects.

"Ya know, that guy who's always sitting by you guys in the morning. The guy who always has those girls hanging on him. The other new kid. I see Aestra and him talking in the hallway a lot."

Jake looks at me again in the mirror, his eyes are questioning me in an almost accusatory way.

"Malek?" I ask. "Are you talking about Malek Forcas?"

"Yeah, yeah! He's really good-looking too."

"No, definitely not Malek! He and I are complete opposites."

"Well," she continues, "seems like he likes you the way he's always staring at you."

I fidget with the strands of hair that have escaped my bun. The last thing I want is for people to start making a

connection between Malek and me. I don't want the suspicion and attention drawn my way. "He does? I... I haven't noticed."

Summer pulls into the parking garage of the apartment complex. "And you know what they say, Aestra? Opposites attract! I bet the two of you would make a perfect couple. I thought it was kind of obvious that he was into you!"

Jake rolls his eyes in the mirror. I don't think he knows I saw him do that.

"Well, it's not obvious. Not to me," I say.

"Don't you think he likes her, Jake?" Summer whines.

"Hey, what do I know? I'm just a guy," he says, dismissing her and the topic of conversation. Summer gives his arm another swat, and we get out of the car.

Vic greets us at the door with beer cans in hand. Summer's eyes beam as she quickly reaches for one and pushes her way through the sea of people. Loud music pumps throughout the spacious apartment, and the main living room area is jam-packed with students from our school. Vic holds out a beer can toward me, "Drinking tonight, girl?"

I shake my head. He tightens his lips in a demeaning sneer, "What about you, cupcake?" he says offering the drink to Jake.

Jake hesitates for a second and then takes the beer. "Summer's gonna have fun tonight, but one can't hurt me." He pops open the can and hurriedly slurps up the rising foam.

Vic pats him on the back. "Good times, man. Good times," he says as he walks among the crowd.

I am tense. Uneasy. Not because of all the underage drinking but because I'm seriously questioning what I'm even doing here. *I can't compete with this crowd.*

"I'm gonna find the bathroom real quick," I say.

"Down the hall to your right," Jake says pointing in the general direction and returning his attention to guzzling his drink.

I don't need to use the bathroom, but I figure it's a safe enough place to hide out for a while. As I reach the door, there's a tap on my shoulder. "What's the story, Morning Glory?" Malek purrs in my ear.

"I figured you would be here," I say as I turn on my heels.

He grabs my hands and leads me away from the bathroom door. "Come with me. Let's chat." I don't want to talk to him. I shouldn't talk to him, but after what Summer said in the car, a new curiosity about Malek Forcas has sprung up inside me. I let him guide me into one of the bedrooms off the hallway. He shuts the door behind us and sits me down on the bed. "How's everything going?" he says.

"Fine," I answer without making eye contact.

"Don't look fine to me. Trouble in the mission?"

"Mission's great," I snap. "What do you want to talk about?"

"You're right, Aestra. You can't compete," he says, and his use of my very own words freezes me in place. I've lost my breath, and I'm struggling to regain control. My hand shakes slightly, and like any predator sniffing out a weakness in its prey, he notices and smirks.

"How did you...?" I stammer.

"No worries," he says. "But you're right. Your mission seems so easy, but you fail to see the influence of the human mind and soul. Like I said, and correct me, but I believe you said it yourself, you can't compete ... not with Vic—he and Jake have been close like brothers for years; not with Europe—the human soul's thirst for adventure and exploration far exceeds the need for stability and routine; not with Summer—her female aspects..." He stops and stares at me as if he's stumbled upon something he hadn't thought of before, but I doubt that. I doubt that anything he says or does is anything less than calculated. His demonic nature forbids him to leave any stone unturned, and the wary pause he's given is a dead giveaway that he's trying to plant a thought in my head.

Ignoring his deliberate silence, I urge him on. "Continue," I say.

"Well, you know you are a female. An interesting pairing from The Powers That Be, don't you think?"

"How so?"

"Well, it's just that in all of my experiences, The Powers would match like-for-like, angel to human, same sex. Yours is a tale quite interesting."

He's frustrating me, and at this point, I think I really do need to use the bathroom. I get up from the bed. "If you have nothing worthwhile to say, then I'm done here."

He grabs my wrist and pulls me back onto him. I stumble into his lap, and he cradles me in his arms for a moment, staring lovingly into my eyes. I try to blink quickly so as to not be entwined within the gray storm of his eyes again, but when I look at them there's a forest—deep and wide and teeming with gentle woodland creatures. His touch is icy; the coolness of his skin seeps through the thickness of my sweater. I hear laughter outside the door of the room, and I try to move, but I can't... I'm dancing with the forest animals with ritualistic movements that sweep me deeper and deeper into the silver light of the moon dazzling in his eyes.

The door bursts open, and my trance is broken. Summer stands in the threshold, drink in hand, and nearly collapses when she sees me embraced in Malek's arms.

"Whoops!" she slurs. "Wrong room! Get him, Big A!" She clumsily fumbles with the door behind her. It was surprising that she could be on her way to a drunken stupor in less than twenty minutes.

I release myself from Malek's hold and scramble to the other side of the bed. "What in the hell was that?" I say.

He reaches into his jeans pocket and takes out a small brown pouch. "Listen," he says softly. "You can compete. You can be successful. This is how." Within the pouch is a medal. It is diamond-shaped, like the one he wears around his neck, except it is flat and pure silver. He dangles the medal in front of my face, and I watch it sway back and forth like a hypno-tizing pendulum. I mindlessly reach for it, but he snatches it up onto its chain and puts it securely back in its bag. "For you," he says, handing me the pouch. "Keep it safe. And only use it when you need to. Your guy, up there," and he points toward the ceiling, referring to Camael, "he watches you, you know, but when you take this medallion out of its bag, he won't be able to see. It's what I call a cloaking device. Pretty, isn't it? I forged this one myself. When you take it out of the bag and hold it, or wear it, you become enshrouded in an invisible aura, so none of those looky-loos from on high can see you. Kinda neat, eh?"

I hold the bag in my unsteady hand. I'm shaking so hard; I might drop it. "I don't want this," I say, and hold my hand out for him to take it back.

He takes my fingers and gently folds them over the bag. "Trust me," he says.

Trust him?

"No, really, it's..."

"Aestra, you're going to need this. There's no other way. You've only begun to crack the surface with your calling. You've just started, and that's fine and everything, but in reality you don't have much time. Jake's going to have to make a decision at some point and..."

I try to back away, but he pulls me toward him again. "And these things take time," I say. "Besides, I know what you are! There isn't anything that you could say or do that would make me trust you. Would you let go of me now?"

He breaks hold of his grip, and the pouch falls to the bed. "You're not the only one invested in this mission, Aestra. There's a lot at stake here. More than you can ever realize."

More mind games? "Yeah, then explain to me how a cloaking device is going to make this all work out?"

"It will give you leverage. You thought it yourself... You will do anything possible to succeed and to help the creation that you and your Lord and your brethren love so much. Consider this an opportunity, an ... advantage. Think of the freedom you'll have when you don't have a giant set of eyes constantly watching you. You'll have freedom to say or do whatever it will take with your ... female accents..."

"You're disgusting."

"Well, I speak the truth. Are you really going to deny the attraction you have for Jake?"

I don't respond because I want him to leave. I want to leave. My eyes remain fixated on the bed, on the brown leather pouch, on the possibilities this could possibly open up for me.

He swipes at my forehead with the back of his hand. The ice sensation of his flesh sends goosebumps down my arms. I shudder from the frigid touch. "And I'll tell you this much... don't have yourself so convinced that all those early morning meetings are just for some class project.

I can't help but look up at him with curiosity.

He huffs as if he just told me something that I should have known all along. Like some idiot who is just figuring out some simple mystery. Who stole the cookie from the cookie jar... duh! "Aestra," he exhales in a near disappointment, "you're so much smarter than that." He leans over, kisses me on the forehead, and leaves. I look down, and the brown pouch has returned to my hands.

CHAPTER TWELVE

——◆—◇—◆——

THE MEDALLION

The loud music from Vic's apartment continued on into the early morning. It's not surprising when at 2:00 a.m. the police came to break up the festivities. What is surprising is that no one got in trouble for the illegal activities that had been taking place! Apparently, Vic knows the officer who was dispatched to his home, and he let everything slide with a blind eye. When the police arrived, Jake took the cue, and we left, dragging Summer in her inebriated condition to her Range Rover. I helped him lay her down in the backseat, and he admonished her not to puke, reminding her that her father will kill her if there was vomit in the car.

He drove Summer home first, walked her to the front stoop of her brownstone, helped her as she fumbled for her house keys, and kissed her goodnight on her cheek. I heard him tell her that he would drop her car off tomorrow morning, and she responded with an incoherent mumble.

She tripped trying to shut the door, and I couldn't help but laugh.

"Next stop," he says when he gets back into the driver's seat, "Aestra's house."

"She okay?" I ask, thumbing my finger toward Summer's house.

"Ah, she will be. She won't feel too good tomorrow morning, probably won't remember much about tonight, but she'll be back to her normal, cheery self bright and early Monday morning. It's Summer's pattern. She's a party girl, and she parties hard."

That's a good thing, as I pray she won't remember seeing Malek and me in our compromising position. "Sounds like you know Summer all too well."

A light drizzle coats the surface of the windshield, and Jake flicks the wiper handle up. "Yeah. I've known Summer since kindergarten. Vic, too. We all grew up together."

"Oh," I say, and that feeling of not being able to compete starts to creep up on me. They're practically a family. They're joined by time and common experiences like Revalia and me. There's no way I'll be able to break through those bonds. I cross my right leg over my left and place my arms in my lap. Against my right elbow, the bulge of Malek's brown pouch presses against my tight jeans. *Consider this an opportunity, an ... advantage.* "So," I continue, "have you and Summer always..."

He shakes his head quickly. "No, no! It's always been an on-and-off thing with us. For years, we've gone back and forth, but it wasn't until the beginning of this senior year that we've been pretty steady."

A stabbing sensation grips my chest again, and I look down. "Oh," I say.

"But, ya know, it's weird though. She's got her head in a different place... if that makes any sense. She's a good person and all, but she has different, um, goals than I do, I guess."

"I understand. She has the party-girl mentality."

"Exactly. I'm kinda beyond all that, ya know?"

"And Europe?"

"Of course, that was all Summer's idea. She's been plotting and planning since the seventh grade to do this backpacking trip after senior year. It was a great idea when we were kids and all, but..."

"NYU," I interrupt.

The rain comes down a little harder; I can no longer count the droplets that ping against the car roof. He puts the windshield wipers on an intermediate setting. "Right. When I got the scholarship, it put a damper on my European dreams. I don't think they'll hold it for a year."

The rain haze makes the street lamps look like mechanical angels with a pulsating electric aura; they remind me of the task at hand. "Can't Europe wait?" I ask.

"Not for Summer," he says abruptly. "When she has her mind set on something, there's no stopping her or telling her no!"

We're getting closer to my house, and I am defeated. This isn't getting anywhere. I'm failing by the second, and then my arm brushes up against my leg, and I touch the bump beneath. Even if I did use the amulet, what would I do with it? And why would shielding my actions from Camael be at all beneficial to me?

"Ya know, Jake, I guess the bottom line really is this: What do you want to do?"

He stops at a red light, takes his hands off the wheel, and runs his fingers through his short hair. "There's a part of me that is all about going to Europe with them. I want to travel, and see the world, and write poetry in Dutch coffee houses. Then the other part of me really wants to settle down, go to school, get my degree, and start a career. Maybe get into journalism, or writing of some type, teaching maybe."

The light turns green, and he goes about half a block before we're in front of my house. He pulls over at the curb and parks the car. The car is still running, and I take it as my sign to get out. I turn to open the door, but the rain pounds down even heavier, and he stops me. "Wait," he says.

"My house is right there; I'm not gonna melt!" I smile.

He turns the ignition off. "Just wait 'til it lets up a little, okay?" he insists.

I shrug my shoulders and turn back around, "Okay."

"What do you think?" he asks. "What do you think I should do?"

I fidget. I can't outright come out and tell him what to do because it doesn't work like that, but since he's asked... "I don't know, I mean, I'm not in your situation."

He rolls his eyes. Apparently, that wasn't a good answer for him. "You know what I mean," he huffs. "Let's say you were."

"Honestly? All I know is that NYU is a pretty penny, and I would have killed to get a free ride. Europe's been around for a very long time, and I don't think it's gonna go anywhere in four years."

He laughs, "That's exactly what I was thinking. You're lucky that you have a solid plan, ya know. You know what you want out of life, and you're determined to get it. You're talented and goal-orientated, and that's admirable. "

"Thanks," I say as I let out a small laugh.

An uncomfortable silence creeps in between us. I concentrate on the rain hitting the car in a rhythmic way; it's like a song longing to have words written for it. Jake is staring at

me, and I fidget again by cracking my fingers. The sound is almost deafening against the stillness in the car.

"It would break Summer's heart if you didn't go, wouldn't it?" I say, breaking the silence.

"Yeah," he says, "but at what cost? And I'm not sure if that even matters anymore." He's still staring at me, his eyes blazing right through me like they did the first moment I located him at school, the first time I saw him from The Observatory. He's looking through my heart and through my soul. I try to crack my knuckles again, but I'm all out of cracks! No matter how hard I bend my fingers back, there's nothing left to pop. My fingers start to get sweaty from my tight grip. He shifts in his seat, facing me now. The jagged light from the street lamp distorts his face with shadows of raindrops. I am enamored with the beauty of his face, the gentleness of his smile, and the soul burning behind his eyes.

"What do you mean?" I say.

"Summer's a nice girl... a great girl, don't get me wrong. But I know she's not for me. We have a good time together, have a lot of memories together, but I don't see it going anywhere beyond that, ya know... like in the future."

"That's okay," I say. "People come in and out of our lives, and..." I pause because I don't really know what I'm saying, and to be quite honest, I don't think he's even listening to me.

"Who's your favorite poet?" he asks.

"What?"

"Answer the question. Who's your favorite poet?"

A no-brainer question, I don't even have to think about this one. "Poe."

"Of course, it would be."

"What are you talking about, I don't understand the..."

"The fact that you even know who Poe is..."

"You can't be serious..."

"Summer had no clue who Poe was, and when I explained it to her she said, 'Oh, that bird guy!' So, just for the record, Poe is the Bird Guy."

This makes me laugh as I uncross my legs and turn to face him directly. "What about you? Who's your favorite poet?"

"The Bird Guy," he responds without missing a beat.

"Figures as much," I say with a smile. Because it would. It figures that there's one more thing driving us together, one more thing connecting our common bonds. "Who knows? Maybe you'll go to NYU, and we'll take a class on Poe together," I joke.

"Yeah, that's exactly what I was thinking," he says, and the car gets awfully quiet again.

I look down and listen to the rain. It's not letting up, not anytime soon, that's for sure. "I should get going."

"Stay a few more minutes," he says, touching my knees.

I hesitate but nod my head. "All right." There's a strange tension building between us. The pit of my stomach feels like it's on a rollercoaster ride, and my heartbeat is a little faster than usual.

"Where are you from?" he asks, moving his hand up my leg.

I pull back a little. His question takes me off guard because he already knows I'm from California, and I certainly can't ever say the word Ilarium 'cause it would make him think I was some kind of nut-job. I raise my eyebrows in response to both his question and his slowly moving hand. "You know where I'm from."

"But, I know you," he says. "I don't know from where, or how, but I know you." I close my eyes and shake my head.

"That's impossible," I mumble.

"I feel like there's something about you that's so strange."

"Oh, gee, thanks," I say sarcastically.

"No... I don't mean you're strange, well..." And his voice trails as he smiles at me again.

"Shut up!" I snap back.

He laughs as he presses his fingers against my right thigh, against the brown leather pouch within my pocket. "What's that?" he asks, smoothing his hand over the bump.

I freeze for a second, my mind scrambling for an excuse, an alibi, a story about the mysterious bag. "Oh, just my necklace," I say, lying so easily. "I didn't know if I should wear it or not tonight, and I..."

"Kept it in your pocket all night? You don't think that's strange?" he teases.

"It's a girl thing, you wouldn't understand... or maybe you do..." I tease back.

He playfully pinches my thigh, and I flinch.

Without realizing that I'm even doing it, I reach into my pocket and take the necklace from the pouch, careful not to touch the medallion. I dangle the silver amulet between us; it catches glints of the artificial streetlight in a prismatic fashion. He is entranced with it; I am too. "It's different. Why don't you wear it?" he says, his eyes trained on the diamond-shaped pendant. And as if being guided by unseen hands, I dip my head into the loop of the chain, the medal bounces once off the center of my chest before nestling between my breasts.

Its power is strong—it envelopes me like a heavy blanket. I'm paralyzed, yet weightless at the same time. The energy surges through every part of me, putting every hair on my body at attention. There are sounds in my ears that both frighten and thrill me at the same time. Malek's voice, Malek's true demon voice, is whispering to me. He speaks in tongues, in riddles, in languages only my angelic nature would be able to translate. But it soothes me, calms my senses, tickles my brain, and shoots throbbing sensations down my spine and...

"See," Jake says. I snap back into the present, wondering how long my attention had drifted away. "It's very pretty. Where did you get it?"

Where did I get it? What do I say? I'm so lost in the essence of Malek's power that I am fuzzy and light-headed like a drunken Summer.

"Family heirloom," a voice whispers in my head. Malek's human voice.

"It's a family heirloom," I say.

"On your father's side," the voice whispers again.

"It came from my father's side of the family," I repeat.

Jake slides closer to me. He gives me an empathetic look, the kind that only he can give me; the kind that says he knows my pain, he knows my loss, he knows that any gift from either of our parents is to be cherished and celebrated until we die. His sweet, golden brown eyes are filled with such understanding. It's hard to resist being drawn into them.

"A beautiful gift for a beautiful girl," he says, and he leans into me.

The moment his lips touch mine, the energy from the necklace engulfs him as well, and I am completely swept away in the warm blanket of energy, Malek's gentle whispers in my head, the kiss, and the rain thrashing against the car.

CHAPTER THIRTEEN

REPERCUSSION

Monday mornings are never fun, especially when the weekend that preceded it was filled with so much activity. The process of waking up and starting the routines of the week all over again can be so tiresome. What's even worse than a Monday morning is a Tuesday morning because you've already completed the first leg of the week, and by the time you relax, go to sleep, and wake up again, you rise the next day thinking, "Oh, God, it's only Tuesday!" and the gloom of the next four days ahead is so depressing. I don't want to think about Tuesday, or Wednesday, or Thursday for that matter. The only day I keep replaying in my head is Sunday. Early Sunday morning in Summer's red Range Rover with the rain gently rapping, rapping on the car door.

Jake called me at 5:00 a.m. this morning, a half hour before my alarm was set to go off, and canceled our morning meeting at the café. Apparently, Summer's Chihuahua was hit by a car yesterday and had to be put down. She was distraught, and Jake stayed with her the whole night for moral support. All of the Lord's creations are sacred; I can understand the bond that Summer must have had with her pet, and I feel bad that she lost her animal companion, but that twinge in the center of my chest struck me deep when he said the words "stayed all night with her." He said he was too tired to think straight and was probably going to skip first and second periods.

Neither of us mentioned the kiss. While it's been weighing heavily on my mind, it's just as well that we didn't talk about it. Anything verbalized could be overheard by Camael, and I've been wrestling with my emotions about the situation non-stop.

There are four distinct aspects at play here. There's Camael and the order of things. I feel guilty because he warned me about barriers and crossing lines. Angels do not have romantic feelings, end of discussion. The love that angels feel is all-encompassing—there's no distinction between the types of love, the categorical division of love. Humans comprehend the notion of love and distribute those feelings into different classifications. "I love my mother" is a much different type of love than "I love the sunset" or "I love my country." And then, of course, there's the frivolous "I love pizza!" or "I love you, man!" which is drastically different than "I love my soul-mate, my life partner, my lover." So, the guilt I'm feeling for having had a romantic incident is my angelic instinct screaming bloody murder at my human soul. But I'm technically human, right? In my fabricated existence, I've had boyfriends and encounters in the past, right? I've kissed boys before and felt that rush of desire before. So, doesn't this align with my natural human existence?

Secondly, and most importantly, Jake is my calling, and I must do what I have to do to complete my mission, right? If what Malek said was true, then playing up the romantic elements of the boy-girl relationship is only the natural progression of things I need to do in order to get the job done. So, I'm probably within the bounds of my limitations. A kiss is just a kiss. No big deal. I know I can't get involved with him much further than just a kiss, but if just a kiss is going to be the way to reach him and get him on the path The Powers That Be need him to get on, then it's okay... Right? Complete the mission. Pass the assignment. Make everything right in the world. Most importantly, help the Creator with his most precious design. If just a kiss is going to set the course of the human race on track, I'll be happy to do just a kiss a thousand times over for the Lord. But again, I'm technically human. Right here, right now. And there's the humanness of me that feels the attraction to Jake on the mental, and yes, I'll admit it, physical level. And I can recognize that it began when I first saw him in The Observatory. There's no guilt or shame in admitting that. In The Observatory, I was drawn to the beauty of his eyes as I would have been to any human's in that up close and personal moment. It was no secret that Aestra, the angel, was fascinated by all humankind.

However, and this is the third aspect at play, something happened to Aestra, the human. My fascination morphed somehow. Maybe my emotions did cross a barrier of sorts? It's just that Jake has touched a part of my soul that makes me feel like I would do anything for him—anything to keep him safe and on the right path. Though, it wouldn't be just for me or my mission but for him because I care about him as a person and not just an assignment. He's touched a part of my heart that awakened a piece of my human aspect. I want to keep him safe, yes. I want to keep him happy, yes, but

I also want to keep him for myself. Summer. She intertwines their arms and kisses him affectionately and says things like, "Hey, babe!" in her high-pitched baby voice. I know she's not the one for him. He even said it himself, but I could have told him that from day one. There's no future there for Summer and Jake. She's not his one. Yet, a slice of my heart is starting to want me to be the one, and I think it's possible that is where my guilt is stemming from ... Malek.

My last point brings me to someone who is supposed to be my sworn enemy. It's not the guilt of a kiss because I pretty much justified all that; I've reconciled my actions in that regard. But what I haven't reconciled is Malek and the amulet. Because if what I did (a kiss is just a kiss) was okay and within my boundaries, I would not have used the medallion to shield my actions from The Powers That Be. That's the most difficult to answer. Why did I do that? And more importantly, how is Camael going to react when he finds out?

So, basically, it's now 5:45 a.m., and I have no motivation to do much of anything. My thoughts have worn me down, and I'm tired and not willing to start the first leg of the usual five-day stretch. I decide I'm not going to school. Aunt Ruth will have to call me in sick or something, and if she doesn't want to do it, then I'll do it myself. One more lie isn't going to get me cast out of Ilarium, that's for sure.

"Aestra," Aunt Ruth calls from down the hall, "you up and ready yet?"

"Not going," I yell back.

Seconds of dense silence hang in the second-story hallway. I know what she's thinking, suspecting. "You sick?" she says, but the lilt of her honey voice indicates that she already knows the answer.

"No."

Some more silence, then she says, "You'll call it in, right?"

I throw my head into my pillow in frustration. I knew she wouldn't do it! "O-kaaa-ay!" I fully expect to hear her high heel shoes click-clacking on the hardwood floors, but there's no sound. She's still standing there, probably in the threshold of her door, hand on hip, contemplating her next sentence.

"Sure you're not sick?" she reiterates.

"Yep."

"Then, meet me for lunch in the city. Lenny's in Times Square. 12 o'clock." She shuts her door and click-clacks down the stairs.

That was not a request... that was a directive. Just when I thought I'd be able to have the day to rest my over-loaded mind...

I take the ferry from Brooklyn to Manhattan. It's practically an all-day affair because I have to catch buses across Brooklyn to get to the pier, and then more buses to get across Manhattan to get to the restaurant. I could have taken a more direct route, but I enjoy the scenery of the ferry ride, especially on this gray, late February afternoon. The city skyline is breathtaking, and I remember that, even as a child, I was completely mesmerized by city life.

Aunt Ruth is already here. As soon as I open the door of the restaurant, I see the back of her blonde hair, pinned up in a professional-looking twist. It's 11:43 a.m. The clock hangs over the pizza counter. I wonder how long she's been here.

She greets me with a hearty hello, but I can tell this isn't a friendly-lunch-date-with-a family-member type of outing. She motions to the chair across from her. "Sit down," she smiles.

I do. Food has already been ordered. Mozzarella sticks and fried calamari—typical Italian fast-food items. "Been here long?" I ask as I reach for a fried calamari ring.

She shakes her head. "Not too long. Things were slow today, so I thought I'd come over and order. You take the ferry?"

"Uh huh. It wasn't too bad. All the buses were running on time so..."

"That's good," she cuts me off. "You okay?"

"Yeah. Fine. Why?"

"It's not like you to ditch school like that, and yesterday, you were pretty quiet up there in your room all day."

She speaks to me like an aunt would. Like this is normal. Like this is your average human interaction between an adult and her adult niece. But there's nothing normal about Ruth and me. She's even less human than I am, and we are by no means your average family. I want to skip the pretense, break through the formalities, and get to the point before my mozzarella sticks get any colder.

"I've had a lot on my mind," I say. "Still adjusting, I guess."

"Listen," she says, and her tone becomes all business in a hot second. "I know about the blackout. I got word from Camael. You're being too risky, Aestra. You're taking too many unnecessary chances, and Camael is in a mood like I've never seen before. He has a hidden agenda, Aestra."

A piece of fried mozzarella crunches in my mouth. "Cam?" I ask, stupidly.

"No," she barks. "You know who I'm talking about. The second you knew what he was, the second you sensed what he was, you should have never entertained anything he had to say to you."

Malek.

She's referring to my interactions with Malek. Camael knows about the amulet.

"What was the harm in talking to him?" I ask.

As the fingers of her right-hand ball up into a frustrated fist, every knuckle cracks. "Harm? Do you not see the harm he has already done? How did he do it? How did he get you to..."

"He didn't do anything," I say. "I did it myself. It was my choice." I'm not quite sure, but I either did the noble thing and accepted responsibility for my actions, or I just defended a demon. I'm afraid of the latter choice.

"Yes, and had you not given him the honor of your precious time, that choice would not have even been there to tempt you. Tell me how it happened."

I reach into my jacket pocket and take out the pouch. "It's a necklace," I admit without removing the pendant from the bag. "It's a veiling device."

Her eyes go so wide and wild; I swear, I think they're going to bulge out of her face. "You have to get rid of it," she urgently whispers.

"I can't," I say matter-of-factly. "I tried."

"Then you have to give it back to him."

"I can't. I tried that too. It always comes back to me. It always somehow ends up in my backpack, or my coat pocket, or my..."

She wipes her nose with her napkin. "Then you have to ignore it. You can't use it again. No good can ever come from it. It blocked you out from Camael's view for a certain length of time, but it's not like Camael didn't see anything... he saw blackness, like when a TV station gets blacked out for a few minutes. It didn't alter time or splice together pieces of time. The blackness bothered him very much. He knew something was wrong." She reaches for my hands, but I ignore her and continue to gorge on my fried foods. "Don't you see? He's a demon, Aestra. A master deceiver, a child of the Father of Lies. A demon is all knowing... brazen, confident, manipulative, a tempter, a seducer. Steer clear of him. Please, I beg you."

My cell phone vibrates in my pant leg pocket, and I take it out to see who's calling. It's a text message from Jake.

[Jake: Where are you?]

I quickly text back and turn my attention back to Aunt Ruth.

[Me: City]

"What happened during the blackout?" she asks.

I realize I might as well come clean. I have no reason to hide the truth. The only thing I may have done wrong was using the amulet, but in the end, what happened between Jake and me was completely justified.

I receive a new text message from Jake.

[Jake: I know... where?]

[Me: Lenny's]

"Would you stop playing with that thing and talk to me?" she scolds. God, she sounds so much like my mother.

"Okay," I say. "He kissed me." And again, her eyes bulge out of her skull. "Just hear me out, though. This is a good approach. I'm making progress with him, and if it goes in this direction..."

"You'll fail if you take it too far!" she gasps. "That's not how things are..."

"Wait. Don't freak out. I see it like this: I need to do everything in my power to get this done right, right?" I pause, waiting for her to say something, or nod, or even grunt, but the only sound is my phone vibrating with another text from Jake:

[Jake: On my way]

But I don't respond because I'm too distracted by Aunt Ruth's eyes that are blazing right through me. I respectfully turn off my phone.

"No, Aestra," she says firmly. "Absolutely not. This can't lead anywhere but to a dark and lonely place for you. I can't even imagine what the consequences would be if..."

"Nothing will happen!" I assert. "I swear! I have this under control. I can do this. Like, think about it... if committing mass murder would bring on world peace, wouldn't you do it?"

As soon as the words escape my mouth, I freeze.

She freezes. Gapes. Mouth opened. Mine is too. The words came out too quickly, like there was no control. I just said. I just rattled on. She breathes in and exhales so loudly that I think everyone in the restaurant heard her. "You heard what you just said, right?" she says calmly.

I nod my head, ashamed.

"You still think you have this under control?"

I don't have an answer. If I can't even control my words, how can I control my actions? She didn't even give me the benefit of the doubt, and...

"Think about this conversation, please. Get home safely. We'll talk later."

$$-\mathfrak{X}-\mathfrak{X}\!\ast\!\mathfrak{X}-\mathfrak{X}-$$

I wander around the city in a fog for a few hours before getting on all my connector buses and heading back to the pier. The boat is in the distance, about a mile out, so I have some time to kill before it docks. The pendant is tucked away safely in its bag in one jacket pocket, and my phone is secured in the other. I take the phone out to check the time when I realize I forgot to turn it back on before.

"What the hell, man?" Jake's voice echoes across the pier.

I turn my head to see him coming toward me. He's holding out his cell phone in one hand and throwing up the other in a "Huh?" gesture.

"What's going on?" he shouts again.

"Jake?" I say in disbelief. "What are you doing here?"

"I told you I was on my way to Lenny's, but when I got there, you were gone. Then you don't pick up your phone. I'm calling you all day, chasing you down. I finally get a hold of your aunt, and she says to try here."

I shake my head with confusion. "What are you talking about?"

"I went to your locker right before third period. That guy Malek was there too. I guess he was wanting to talk to you about something. Anyway, he said you texted him that you were going to the city to see your aunt."

"I didn't..."

He comes closer to me. "Uh, yeah, you did. He showed me the text. So, I went to the nurse, checked myself out sick, and got on the train."

A demon is all-knowing... ain't that the truth! But the bigger issue here is Jake actually followed me. Tried to track me down all over Manhattan. My brain is still trying to process. "Why the seek-and-rescue mission, commander?" I joke.

"I don't know. I felt bad about bailing on you this morning over a stupid friggin' dog. And then when I heard you were out for the day, I thought it would be cool to hang out, maybe get something to eat, and get some work done. I'm almost finished with the project, and I wanted to run some ideas by you."

Project? He wants to talk about the project. He came all the way to the city to find me to discuss an assignment for class? "Wow, you're really into this project, aren't ya?"

"I gotta get an 'A,' ya know?"

I suppose so. I pull my jacket tighter around my neck as the wind picks up a little. The boat is getting closer to the pier. I watch as it cuts through the dark waves in the harbor, and I let the sounds of the water consume me. Tuning out Jake's presence, I absorb the distant ring of dingy bells, the smell of the fuel engines polluting the air, and the silence of two awkward human beings who have so much to say to each other but choose not to speak. Is he watching and hearing the same things as I am, or is he thinking about Europe with Vic and Summer?

Jake fidgets with something in his pocket, breaking my daydream. "Ya know the other night when we were on the phone, and you said that you wouldn't let me read your poetry unless I let you read mine first?"

I nod.

"Well, here," he says handing me a piece of folded paper. "I want you to read this."

I take the paper from him, unfold it, and read the title. "'Aestrangel'? What's this?"

"Just read it," he says.

And I do.

And the world stops turning, and my heart stops beating, and the dingy bells stop ringing, and the waves stop crashing, and I am motionless and speechless and helpless and confused and utterly stunned.

"I can't figure you out, ya know?" he begins. "I've been friends with lots of girls, dated lots of girls, and I always thought I had a pretty good handle on chicks. But you're so different. Strange. Even your name is so weird. But through all that strangeness, I feel like I know you somehow. I feel like I've known you my whole life, and at the same time, I have no idea who the hell you are."

I laugh because he's right. I've felt the same way about myself as well, but for vastly distinct reasons, of course. He says these words as if he's rehearsed them, as if he's spent all day thinking about... oh, yeah... he probably did! He had all day to catch up with me! And here I was wondering why we hadn't talked about the kiss from the other night. I fold up the poem and put it in my jacket pocket next to the brown pouch.

The ferry docks at the pier, and the bell rings. People start to disembark and scatter on the wooden dock like ants marching. Jake lifts my chin and leans down to kiss me. An electric surge races through my arms and chest. People bump into us. Their angered voices grumble that we're standing in their way. I clasp the poem, and my fingers brush up against the pendant's case. I can almost hear Malek urging me to take it out of the pouch and hold on to it tightly. I remember the swoon I felt from the energy it possesses, but I ignore its power because the power of my own self-confidence is far stronger than Malek's magic toy and the power of my own self-esteem has risen up above me, above the crowd of people swarming around us, and above the heavens of Ilarium. I don't care who bumps into me. I don't care who sees me now.

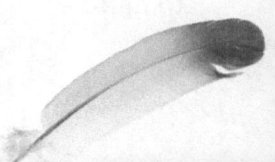

CHAPTER FOURTEEN

CHANGE OF PLANS

"I can make her disappear, ya know?" Malek says calmly. The menacing tone in his voice is hard to ignore, and I roll my eyes at him.

He's referring to Summer, who's sitting with her friends at an adjacent table at the café. Malek has been talk-talk-talking away, and I guess I must have been staring at her something hard. I had been waiting for Jake when Malek made his usual grand appearance. I've been ignoring what he's been saying, for the most part, but his insinuation of doing something to Summer is too much for me to disregard.

"And what would make you think that I would want that?" I say.

"Your jealousy is bleeding through your aura. I was offering a suggestion, Sunshine. Because, you know, I still have most of my power, and it would be a rather easy job to handle."

Most of his power? Kind of unfair that he's able to retain any of his power, when all of my angel abilities have been stripped away. But he said "most," implying that he has more. Maybe his human body is not capable of handling it all. Or, maybe he's lying to me, which I wouldn't put past him. "That is the craziest thing I've ever heard! And I'm not jealous of her!" I snap at him.

"Is it, though? It would solve a lot of your problems if Miss Summer took a fall, or had an accident, or took one too many pills."

"Stop talking like that. As a matter of fact, stop talking. I'm doing fine on my own, thank you very much."

He moves his hand thoughtfully to rub his chin. "Ah, yes, you are, aren't you," he agrees. "Causing quite a stir with the higher-ups. You didn't even use my..."

I dig through my backpack. "Yeah, about that," I interrupt, "take this back. It's useless to me, and I don't want it. I don't know why I let you give it to me in the first place, but I don't need it, so here." I slide the brown pouch across the table.

He chuckles softly. "Oh, Aestra, you know I can't take your family heirloom. It's yours." He slides it back to me. It belongs to you; it always has. And it would deeply hurt my feelings if you gave back a gift, I mean I made it, especially for you, you know," he whispers.

"No really, I..."

"I can't take it back." His voice sounds deeper, more serious. "It's yours. It will always be yours. Whether you use it or not."

I give up. Why I continue this conversation is beyond me. I think the human Aestra is starting to mistake his attention for some kind of strange friendship; the human Aestra is drawn to him and comforted by him. The angel Aestra is screaming on the inside to run far away from him, but there's this irresistible "moth-to-the-fire" sensation that swells inside me whenever Malek is around. "Ya know, I'm not even supposed to be talking to you," I finally say after some silence.

He looks around the room with a sarcastic grin. "But yet, here we are." He's right, and the smile on his face lets me know that he knows it. "It's a double-edged sword, isn't it?" he says.

I'm frustrated and wish that Jake would get here soon. There's a set pattern with Jake and Malek: when Jake arrives, Malek vanishes. When Jake isn't around, Malek appears. I feel like it's a vicious cycle of good and evil between the two most important men in my life. Like, I have to save the good, Jake, obviously, and vanquish the evil, Malek, of course. "What in the world are you talking about now?" I ask with an exasperated huff.

"You know what I mean, Aestra. Your superiors—your beloved Camael, good old Ruthie, they all tell you to 'Get the job done!' and pat you on the back and say 'Go get 'em, tigress' and 'Do everything you can to set that boy on the straight and narrow.' And wouldn't you know, the very moment, the very instant," he snaps his fingers, "you reach the climax of the story where you muster up the courage to actually get the job done, they tell you you're wrong. They tell you you're not doing it the right way. They put restrictions and limitations on you. As if you don't have enough restrictions holding you back. And they call that guidance? They call that purpose? Ya know what I call that? I call that entrapment. I call that a classic bait-and-switch! It's almost as if they're setting you up for failure. Haven't you thought about that?"

I don't answer him, but yes, those thoughts have crossed my mind. And not just my human mind...

"The one I work for, Aestra, the one that I serve, my Lord and Master, he would never be as cruel and deceptive as that. With him, you always know the expectations. With him, you always know the truth."

"Truth?" I say, nearly choking on my coffee. "How can you speak of truth when all that you speak of is nothing but lies and deceptions?"

His face contorts. "Have I ever lied to you, Aestra? Have I ever told you something that turned out to be false? Maybe when the truth is right in front of you, maybe when it's so strong and so 'in your face,' you look beyond that truth and twist it to your own liking, thus creating your own lies."

I don't have a chance to respond because Jake arrives. Finally! He sits next to me in the booth, and I put the brown pouch back into my bag.

"Think about what I said," Malek says before leaving.

I brush my hair from my eyes. "Will do," I say.

"What was all that about?" Jake asks when Malek's out of earshot.

"Nothing," I lie. "He's such a pain in the ass."

Jake laughs. "I think he's trying to kick it to as many girls in the school as he can!" And we both look over to where Malek ended up, and sure enough, it's a table filled with girls from school all giggly and bubbly and fawning all over him. I smile and shake my head dismissively.

I think it odd that Jake sat next to me when he normally sits across from me, but he pulls out his slim-line laptop from his backpack and sets it up on the table. "I wanna show you what I have so far with the project. The PowerPoint is pretty much done; it just needs some cutesy graphics and animations, and..."

"That's where I come in," I answer as the file loads up.

He starts clicking each slide, one after the other. "You got it," he says. "The research that we both did is all there, but it needs something…"

"Extra."

"Exactly."

I scan through each slide, glossing over the information. It looks very comprehensive. The material flows with a good progression, not only highlighting the important poets from each time period but also giving a quick background on world events that served as an influence on the development and evolution of the genre. He is right, though, the presentation is a bit bland, and I know he didn't want to come out and say it in so many words, but it desperately needs a woman's touch.

"I'll play with it," I say. "Spruce it up, make it look appealing to the masses."

"Great," he says as he turns toward me.

We're looking into each other's eyes, and I am dizzy as if the world has stopped spinning and only my body is in perpetual motion. It's like our souls are speaking to one another in their own language. I'm going to get lost here if I don't say something. "I got coffee for you," the words come to my lips and out of my mouth, but they're unintelligible to my ears.

"Thank you," he replies, letting me know that he heard those words, but he never once looks at the table or the cup in front of him. He's looking at me, scanning my face, studying my features. We're locked in our gaze. He raises his eyebrows as if to say "Well, what's next?" and I raise mine in response, nervously biting my lower lip. My body is screaming for his mouth to touch mine with his magical kiss, and suddenly, it's as if all the energy in my body rushes out of me. I am weak and numb with anticipation.

"Whatcha doing?" the baby voice says, breaking into the moment.

I look up to see Summer.

"Hey," Jake says, fidgeting.

There's a glint of worry in her eyes, but she hides her emotions well with a smile. "Oh," she says, "let me guess. Project."

Jake and I both nod our heads. I take a sip of coffee to prevent her from reading anything on my face. She sits down in the exact spot Malek occupied a few minutes prior. Two enemies, I think uncontrollably. "Can I see?" she asks.

"No!" Jake and I say simultaneously. We look at each other and smile. Summer's face darkens.

"Uh-huh," she huffs, "well, excuuuuse me!" She's trying to lighten the mood, but I can tell she's not happy, suspicious even. "Well, babe," she continues, "pass that laptop my way!" She reaches across the table and turns the screen toward her. Her fingers furiously tap the keyboard, and she abruptly stops, waiting for a website to load up. "I wanna show you this great little hostel I found in Vienna. We can have a private room with a view of the courtyard, and Vic could be down the hall. Each room has its own kitchen, and it's in walking distance to downtown." She turns the screen to show Jake, and there it is—a bright and clean hostel with all the amenities a hostel could ever offer. "The price is great, too," she beams.

"Yeah, about Europe," he says slowly. I tense up, unable to move, and I watch Summer's sunny face drop slightly when she picks up on Jake's foreboding tone.

"What about it?" she asks with a serious tone.

"I gotta tell you, Summer, I'm not gonna be able to go."

She drums her nails on the tabletop. "What do you mean? We've been planning this for forever!" she roars.

"Look, I thought about it," he begins to explain, but he struggles for the right words. Underneath the table, I squeeze his knee, letting him know he's doing the right thing, that he's made the right choice. He drops his head and gives me an inconspicuous sideways glance before continuing. "I can't do an entire year. They won't hold my scholarship. If you shortened the trip, or postponed until winter break next year, then maybe I could..."

Summer's head is wildly shaking from side to side. "No! No! No! That's not the plan, Jake. I had to make sacrifices to make this trip happen too, ya know. My job was generous enough to hold my position for the time I'll be away!"

He huffs. "Sum, there's a big difference between your job at the nail salon and my full ride to NYU."

I can't help but smirk. Unfortunately, Summer notices. "Oh," she says, sucking in her anger. "It's got something to do with her, doesn't it?" She points her perfectly manicured finger at me.

Jake and I exchange glances. "No, no," he says, "it's about the money... my scholarship. Europe will always be there, Sum. I can go before school starts in the fall. I can even meet you overseas when I'm on break."

"It won't be the same," she says, tears welling in her eyes, but they're not tears of sadness, they're tears of anger, and maybe something else... jealousy?

"Summer, I..." he starts.

"It's fine. Really. It's fine," she says, wiping the edges of her eyes, her voice dripping with sarcasm. "Vic and I will have to come up with another plan. Go off and get your learn on. Get that big bad English degree. Go off and teach some snot-nosed kids, 'cause what do you do with an English degree, anyway? Certainly, you don't get to see the sights of Europe, now do you?" And she walks away.

My hand tightens on his knee. He places his hand over mine and squeezes back.

I took Jake's laptop to the library after school so that I could put the finishing touches on the project in a quiet environment. Of course, home is a quiet environment, but I didn't want to see Aunt Ruth and have a theological conversation. That would have completely distracted me from the work that had to get done, and with Friday being our due date, I want this project to finally be over with. Not that many kids stay after school, and even fewer hang out in the library, so I felt like I was utterly alone for once. I had even toyed with using the amulet so Camael couldn't spy on me, but I decided against it. That would have been spiteful of me, and I didn't want to upset him any more than I already have, but the thought did amuse me when it entered my mind.

I hit the save button, close up the computer, and stick it in my backpack. The clock now reads 7:30 p.m. It's already dark outside, and I look forward to the nighttime stroll back to the brownstone. When I called Aunt Ruth earlier, she offered to pick me up, but I declined, opting for the chill of the walk to settle into my bones.

And it is chilly! It is rounding early March, and there are still no signs of spring on the horizon. It figures... the one time I get to experience Earth and the Creator's ultimate design, it would have to be during the hard-packed cold of winter. I'm not complaining. It's rather fitting. I'm able to see first-hand the coldness that lies in some humans' hearts... lovelessness, greed, anger, and jealousy. And to think the Creator loves them all, flaws and all, sins and all. He forgives, and forgets, and loves unconditionally. They weren't kidding when they said that humankind was his most complex creation ever!

I scarcely notice the car creeping up slowly next to me, but when I turn my head, I realize it's not just any car… it's Summer's red Range Rover, and it's starting to rain.

The car speeds up and pulls to the curb a few inches ahead of me. The window of the front passenger side slides down with an electric hum, and when I catch up to it with my normal walking pace, Summer leans over the passenger seat. I can't tell if there's anyone else in the car. "Hi, Aestra!" She sings my name, but there's a hint of underlying venom laced in her song.

"Oh, hey, Summer," I say with a small wave as I continue walking forward.

She rolls the car up to meet me. "Hey, it's starting to rain. Do you want a ride home or something?"

Or something?

"Nope. I'm good, thanks."

"You sure?" she asks, but it sounds as if she hesitated for a second. "I mean, I… I'm going your way, and…"

Just then the back door bursts open. Summer sharply pulls the Range Rover to the curb and slams on the brakes. The wheels screech underneath the now slick asphalt. Vic gets out from the backseat and tilts his thick neck to one side. His neck cracks with a sickening sound, and he interlocks his fingers to crack them as well.

"What's your problem?" he asks me, as he comes toward me.

I try to walk calmly away from him, but I'm frozen with fear. "I don't know what you're talking about, Vic."

He walks at an angle and backs me against the Range Rover. If my heart doesn't stop beating so fast, I'll probably have a heart attack. "You're seriously not gonna play dumb with me, are you?"

Run, stupid! Run! I yell at myself from the inside, but there's no response from my legs.

"You think you can come to our school, materialize from out of nowhere, and go messing with our lives?"

"What are you...?" I stammer, afraid.

He puts both arms against the side of the car, boxing me in. Tears rise in my eyes. "Listen," he says, "let's not play dumb, okay?" He leans his wide face closer to mine. There's a smoky scent to his breath, and I tilt my head to the side to avoid another whiff of it. "We all know you got a thing for my boy, Jake. But I don't think anyone gave you the memo that Jake is off-limits!"

Another car door opens, and Summer makes her way to the sidewalk. She pushes Vic's arm aside, and he steps back. She gets up in my face—her eyes are swollen and red from previous tears, and there's a mad-dog snarl painted on her nose and mouth. "Stay the hell away from him, bitch!" she growls under her breath. I try to back up, but there's nowhere for me to go.

"Summer..." I begin, trying to understand, trying to reason with her.

"Don't even try to defend yourself! Your buddy Forcas told me everything—your little trip to the city, your little kiss on the dock. I swear, if I see you even look Jake's way again, I think I will have to kill you!"

There's no talking to her. No reasoning. No trying to make her understand. She's on the edge; her fierce instinct to protect what she thinks is hers is emerging in full-force. "I don't know what Malek told you," I say, "but if you let me explain to you..."

She laughs, and in the street light, I can see more tears streaming down her face. "Explain? Isn't she funny, Vic. She wants to explain why she's hooking up with my boyfriend!"

"Summer, it's not like…"

I see a crack of light before I feel the sting on my face, and my hand instinctively goes up to my cheek. It's wet, and I can't tell if I'm bleeding or if it's the steady rain that is descending upon us. I twist my head to block, anticipating another punch, but none comes. As the ringing sound in my ear fades away, the noises of the city street start to come back into earshot, coupled with the continuous laughter from Vic and Summer.

Something comes over me. I don't know what this feeling is. Rage? Anger? Hatred? It bubbles in the pit of my stomach and radiates throughout my whole body, swelling against the pulsating sensations in my quickly bruising face. It's the feeling that I had that night in The Observatory when Revalia and Lozhure teamed up on me, and I felt lost and helpless in my angelic nature, but now I see red. I see red. I see red.

I see red…

And I'm on top of Summer before I even realize what I've done. I can't see her face through the red veil that has overcome my vision. Her head thuds against the concrete as I mash my elbow against the side of her nose; the bone crunches under my weight. I don't have enough time to do any more damage because, in a flash, Vic grabs me from behind and slams me against the car.

"Are you fucking crazy!?" he screams in my face before crashing his open hand across my mouth.

He's all over me, snarling in my ear, pulling my hair back, exposing my neck. He lifts me easily off the ground by my shoulders and slams me into the side of the car again. The bones in my back crack from the force. He unzips my jacket, and his hands go up my shirt. He is groping me, touching me, tearing at my clothes, grabbing at my every body part. I raise my arms in defense, trying to push him away, but it's no use, he overpowers me. He takes his knee and jabs me between the legs, which causes him to laugh in my ear. He takes his knee again and forces it into my stomach. The wind is knocked out of me, he lets go, and I crumple to the gutter. He walks over to Summer, who's sitting up on the sidewalk. He helps her up and into the car, shoving her in the backseat. He gets in the driver's side and pulls away, leaving me in the gutter, leaving me in the rain.

-PART III-
THE FALLOUT

THE LEVELS OF THE DEMONIC ORDERS

THE 1st ORDER
APOKOMISTAI—THE OLD ONES
Lucifugi – the nocturnal
Subterranean – the underground
Terrene – the land dwellers

THE 2nd ORDER
NEKUDAIMONES—THE YOUNG ONES
Aqueous – the water
Aerial – the air
Emperyal – the atmosphere

"THE EVENING STAR"

Oh, Great One, we bow
In Your presence, at Your mercy;
For You, and You alone,
Can light the blackened sky

CHAPTER FIFTEEN

SEEING RED

The walk back home is staggering; I'm unsteady on my feet and my brain pulsates against my skull. The rain is coming down harder now. My jacket is still open, and I'm getting drenched from the rain. I don't care. I'm freezing, and yet, I don't care.

Slowly, I wander through the dark, wet streets, soaking up the ugliness that is humankind. Have I been wrong all this time? For so long, I had revered this brilliant creation of the Lord, I marveled at their beauty and imperfections, and I sang their praises and wished so badly to serve them and serve them well. And for what? To be violated and beaten up in the street because of jealousy and anger? I was not so naïve to think that these things didn't ever happen. I mean, I've seen the greatest atrocities of humankind unfold before me as I prayed for people's salvation and restoration. But to

me? To happen to me? If they only knew who I really was, then maybe I would have been treated differently.

So, what have I believed in all this time? What did I put my faith so strongly and deeply in? Humankind? With all of its violence, and hostility, and anger, and rage? Is this really what I longed to be a part of... a jealous world where men and women alike have no self-control even over the simplest emotions? But I know, no emotion is ever simple, and every emotion is deeply felt. Being in the thick of it, being able to feel those emotions for myself, has been everything I had ever dreamed it would be, and yet, it is everything I feared. I answered back violence with more violence. My own uncontrollable emotions overtook me—the undeniable feelings that have made me completely human. I'm amazed at how quickly I reacted in response to Summer's punch to my face. It was all reaction. No thought process behind it... just a physical response. Is that the way all humans operate? Is that what really goes on inside the human brain? Feel and act?

Yes. I must have been wrong about people, blinded by my love of the Creator and all that he has made. Camael said that Revalia was tainted with humanity, and at the time, I found his choice of words to be odd. Not so much anymore. I understand why he said "tainted." Humans are imperfect, flawed, and ugly. They are the only species in the entire universe that has the power to destroy itself and the will to do it. They are tainted... tainted with the wisdom of a higher-powered soul trapped in the boundaries of a human body and the inability to reconcile the two.

I wonder if I hurt Summer badly, and a part of me wants to tell her I am so very sorry for how I acted, but then I think about Vic and his prying hands violating me, and a part of me doesn't care about smashing Summer's head against the concrete. But then again, Summer and Vic are humans, and if I were to justify their actions, if I were to reconcile and nearly forgive their actions, I would conclude that they were only feeling and acting upon their strongest, innermost desires. What they did to me tonight was their way of making me "disappear"—the same notion I juggled in my own head this very morning. "I can make her disappear, you know," my adversary had tempted. However, Malek's definition of "disappear" is far more literal than what Summer and Vic deem it to be. "Disappear" to them is "Go away," or better yet, "Stay away." To Malek, I'm afraid, it means something much more sinister.

The lights are off in the brownstone, and I assume that Aunt Ruth is out for the night either late at work, or at dinner with friends. I don't want to go in yet, so I sit on the front stoop. I pull my jacket up over my neck and tuck my face to my knees. It throbs—my whole body throbs. I know my face, from where Summer punched me and Vic slapped me with his lunchbox hand, is blowing up around the bottom of my eye. I should probably get ice on it, but there's something about the pain, something about the sting that's comforting. Perhaps I'm punishing myself for the way I acted, or rather, the way I've been acting.

I hear a car pull up to the curb in front of the brownstone, but I don't look up. Someone gets out of the car, and for a split second, I think it's Summer and Vic coming to beat me up some more, and my heart freezes in anticipation of their callous blows.

"What the hell is going on?" the voice says.

Jake.

He doesn't sound angry or upset. He sounds concerned—worried.

I look up from my jacket, and he winces when he sees my face. "Aestra!" he gasps in disbelief. "What the hell...?"

I touch my cheek. "That bad?" I ask, but I know it is because the side of my mouth has swelled up giving my voice a mumbled sound.

"Summer called me, all hysterical sounding. Something about she knew about me and you and how she punched you out. What the hell did she do to you?"

"Jumped me. I'm sorry, Jake. This is a big mess."

"The only thing that's a mess right now is your face. Let's go inside, please, so you can get out of those wet clothes and get some ice on your face before you blow up like a balloon."

I know he's trying to keep it light, so I give a little chuckle. He helps me up, and I open the door. I was right, Aunt Ruth isn't home, which is for the better because I don't think I would be able to explain what happened to her. We walk upstairs to my room, and I throw my wet jacket to the floor.

"Summer broke up with me," he says as I sit down on the bed and take off my saturated boots and socks.

"I'm so sorry, Jake…"

"Not your fault. It was kinda heading in that direction, but I don't understand how she knew about the city and, well, ya know … the pier?"

"Malek," I say, and my face twitches with pain.

"Forcas? Really? You told him?" His voice sounds a little accusatory.

"No. I think he followed me. I know he followed me. He always follows me."

"I thought you guys were friends."

"We're not. I mean, we are. I mean, it's super complicated."

"Vic put his hands on you, too?"

I close my eyes, remembering what Vic did to me. What Jake means is "Did Vic hit you, too?" Only, Vic did so much more than that, but I fail to mention it. "Yes," I say quietly, and I leave it at that.

Anger fills his face and he slams his fist against the wall of my bedroom. "I'm gonna kill him!" he growls.

"No. Don't say that." I can see how the vicious circle of violence has begun, and I need to find a way to end it.

"Aestra! He hit you. Hit you. What kind of a man ever puts a hand on a woman? That's not right! I gotta take him out."

I get up from the bed, walk over to him, and grab his arms, restraining him from hitting my wall again and possibly putting a hole through it. "No," I say firmly, looking deeply into his eyes. "That's not what I want you to do. I want you to let this go for now. No retaliation. Vic is your best friend, and he made a mistake, a horrible, disgusting mistake. But I forgive him, and you need to forgive him, too. Please, it's what I want."

He stares into my eyes for a few moments. "Why do you have such a good heart?" he asks.

I can't tell him the truth, so I continue to gaze back at him.

"You're soaking wet," he says, breaking our stare. I look down, and yes, I am drenched. "Get your clothes off, and I'll go get you some washcloths to take care of your face. Where's the bathroom?"

I point out the door. "Across the hall."

"Okay." He shuts the door behind him.

I rummage through my closet, find my white robe, and get undressed. The mirror from the vanity table flashes me side glimpses of the hideous face I wear as I remove my soaked clothes and wrap the oversized robe tightly around my waist. I walk closer to the mirror and see that my face isn't just swollen, there's a gash on the corner of my lip, probably from one of Summer's rings, and a small cut underneath my eye. I look like a demon, a revolting, puffy-faced demon with wild abandon in her heart, 'cause let's face it, that's exactly how I acted. Give me some horns, and I know what Malek sees in his mirror every day! I can barely stand to look at myself, this warped reflection of jealousy and hatred staring back at me. I wish I could hide, wish I could erase the monster who emerged from within me, wipe away the bruises and scars, and as the door opens back up, I spy the brown pouch on the vanity's countertop. I pick up the bag and hold it tightly in my hand.

"Freezing water. I think that'll help the swelling," Jake says, closing the door behind him. I reach out with my free hand to take the washcloth from him, but he shakes his head and approaches me. "No," he instructs. "Let me do it."

I stay very still as he gently presses the cold rag onto my bulging face. I wince at the sting of the first touch, but within seconds, the cold sensation envelopes my pulsing flesh, soothing me. He wipes at the two cuts, gingerly patting the one under my eye and dabbing the one at the side of my lip. Through the pain, through the sting of my wounds, I begin to breathe a little heavier. There's a heat from his hands that radiates through the ice cold of the cloth. The warmth and frigidness makes me shiver, a deep bone shake that rocks my whole body.

"Did I hurt you?" he whispers.

"No, I'm fine," I smile. "Thank you."

He smiles back, but not just with his mouth, he smiles with his mysterious eyes. "You're very welcome."

"I must look like a monster," I say through the cloth that's covering my face.

"Not from where I'm standing," he says, and again, my body shivers.

"Well, the messed up side of my face is covered up, ya know?" I answer playfully.

Suddenly, he stops tending to my wounds and lets the rag fall to the floor. He lifts my chin slightly and locks his lips onto mine. The pain from the gash on my mouth sends a wave of discomfort throughout me, but the tenderness in his kiss is soothing—magically alleviating the tension in my head, the throbbing in my face. Again, I'm lost in him. His hand reaches up around the back of my neck, and he draws me closer to him, pulling me into him, kissing me deeply, passionately.

And I kiss him back.

I wrap my arms around his neck, still holding on to the leather pouch, and he breaks our kiss, moving his mouth to my demon face, gently kissing the bruised cheek, my eye lid, and back down to the swollen side lip. His breath, warm on my skin, tickles my aching flesh. He dips his head into the hollow of my neck, and kisses me there, his teeth slightly grazing the bump of my neck bone. I'm swooning, drunk on my own blood rushing throughout my body.

His mouth moves lower onto my chest, below my clavicle, and his hand moves to unfasten the terrycloth belt on my robe. I shiver again. My hands shake, and my knees are locked in place. I feel like I'm falling, falling, falling, as the robe falls passed my shoulders. He brings his head back up to my neck, breathing in my essence every inch of the way up. But suddenly, he stops, and I go cold with fear.

His hand runs up my naked back, and his fingers make their way to the raised scars on my shoulder blades. The scars from my accident. The death of my parents. The death of my angelic self. "Your wings," he whispers in my ear, and I realize my back is facing the mirror in my vanity. He sees them in the reflection, monstrous scars to match my hideous face.

My shoulders rotate to prop the robe back up, and I tug at the opening to close it around me. I don't want him to see the scars. I don't want to have to explain them, or the pain,

or the trauma, because that would mean I would have to lie to him. Again. And I don't want to lie to him.

He stops me and pulls back. We are face to face now, and I'm shaking. I shake from the intense fear and desire and excitement and sadness that fills my heart and washes over me all at once. "They're beautiful," he says looking me directly in the eyes, and in this moment of honesty, I hesitantly pull the robe back down, exposing the extent of my missing wings. The scars are thickly raised above the surface of my back; the dark peach color extends across the entire length of my shoulder blades. He moves my hair to the front of my shoulder and looks at my back in the mirror. He looks amazed, puzzled at how I could have survived such a horrific ordeal, and yet there's a glint of affection in his eye, like he approves of my scars, like he's seeing something that he's longed to see his whole life. It makes me uncomfortable, him staring at me in such a way. I close my eyes in hopes of shielding myself, shielding my shame.

In my moment of weakness, the bag drops from my hand, clanging to the hardwood floor. He steps back, picks it up, and hands it back to me. "Your necklace?" he asks.

I nod my head as I clutch it tight in my hand.

He swipes my hair to the side and down my back and kisses me again, and I'm lost again. I'm his. He pulls me closer toward him, but his arms find the opening of my robe and wrap around my waist. His shirtsleeves are a little damp, and the coldness sends goose bumps across my stomach. As we continue our embrace, continue our kiss, his hands reach up my back, caressing the raised skin of my scars. His touches are so different than the violent ones from Vic. Vic's hands were wrought with hatred and anger. They made me feel dirty and ashamed, but Jake's hands send nothing but good vibes to every inch of my body. His touches are warm and loving, and something that I could get very used to.

In one swift movement, the robe slides off my shoulders, down my arms, and onto the floor. The pulsing in my face has spread to the rest of my limbs, down the trunk of my body, between my legs, and down to my feet.

I can't control this. My desire is too strong to be contained. It was always there, but now, I'm at the precipice of human craving, and I can't turn back. There's no turning back. And quite honestly, I don't want to turn back. I pull away from him, stand before him completely in the flesh. He smiles, but all I can think of is how Camael is not. I'm betraying him. This is the line, and I'm crossing it. I can stop it, I know I can. Right now, I can turn back, tell Jake to leave, choose not to cross the line. But I won't. I don't. I don't want to.

Camael has seen enough.

There's no thought process behind it, just action. I open up the brown leather pouch and dangle the medallion in front of my eyes before looping the chain over my head. I breathe in the energy released from it. It washes over me, in me, through me. I let the darkness within cover me, and then Jake is within its atmosphere as well, kissing me again, touching me again, leading me to the bed where I dreimily collapse under the weight of his body.

CHAPTER SIXTEEN

ALWAYS YOU

The lamplight in my room casts shadows along the walls. They flicker and dance, and somehow, it's as if there are hundreds of tiny demons staring at me with their gray eyes—gray eyes like Malek's, accompanied by shadowy smiles. There's no breeze or opened door, but the medallion, which now hangs from the side of my bedpost, gently sways back and forth, it, too, catching the light of the lamp, it, too, creating ghastly images of the shadow-realm in my room.

Jake lies next to me, sleeping. He had said to let him rest for no more than fifteen minutes, but that was two hours ago. I must have dozed off, as well. His chest rises slowly with each breath he takes, and so I prop myself on one elbow and place my hand on his rib cage feeling the movement of his lungs expanding and collapsing. I could watch him like this for hours, for in his slumber he is even more beautiful. His eyelids flutter, and I wonder what it is he could be dreaming about. Me? What happened here tonight?

I run my hand across the surface of his chest, and goose bumps bloom along the flesh where my fingers graze. I am at peace and wish to stay so. This feeling—my bare skin up against his, my face nuzzled into the crook of his arm, giving him my body and soul—is indescribable. There is a sense of safety in his arms, and a sense of love, because I can love him on multiple levels.

And I can get used to this.

I don't need my powers, my wings, my angelic form to sustain me. I feel the death within my human body on a daily basis, and I welcome it. If it means I could wake up like this—in Jake's life, in Jake's arms—I would gladly and willingly stay.

But I know I can't. I know that's not possible for me.

Because time is running out for me, and I've done something so irreversible that it's a matter of moments before I must face the consequences of my actions. But I wish we could stay like this forever.

This bed.

This moment.

He stirs, but I dare not wake him. I can't wake him, not now. Let him dream, let him rest, let me fantasize about something I can never have because for these few fantastic moments, I have it, and it's real, and it's glorious, and I never want the feeling to go away. I never want to wake from this daydream.

The door opens downstairs and slams with an urgency I recognize. I glance at the clock. It reads 1 a.m. I anticipate Aunt Ruth's heeled shoes clacking up the steps, and when they do, I am overwhelmed with the feeling that she knows. She knows. She knows. I gently tap Jake, rousing him awake.

His eyes open and when they come into focus, he smiles at me. "Hey sleepyhead," he whispers dreamily. I can't help but smile back.

"I fell asleep, too," I say. "It's late. Like, really late. My aunt just got home."

"Oh, shit!" he says, grabbing for the blankets.

"Shhh," I urge as the *clack-clack* gets closer.

He rolls over onto his side, facing the wall. I get under the covers and position my body to try to conceal him as best as I can. My bedroom door opens wide, and I can sense Aunt Ruth standing silently in the doorway, the tension is built up so thick, I can barely breathe.

"Aestra," she says calmly, and I dig my fingers into the side of Jake's thigh. "It's late. You need to send your friend home. Now."

She leaves, shutting the door behind her. Jake and I say nothing. I know whatever words are exchanged between us in the next few moments will be our last.

He turns over to face me. "You heard the general," he whispers. "I probably should get going."

I don't answer him. I can't. My stomach twists and turns, and I can't help the tears that stream down my face.

He wipes at my eye with his thumb. "No. None of that. It's fine. So she'll yell at you for having a boy in your bedroom. She'll ground you or something. No big deal. Life will go on," he tries to reassure me, but he doesn't know the extent of it. Life will go on, for sure. For me, for him... yes, life will go on... without each other, though, because I'll be getting more than grounded the second Jake walks out the front door. I suck down the tears and sniffle. "See, no biggie," he smiles his irresistible smile.

I claw at his shoulders. "Don't leave me," I beg.

His lips purse, and he chuckles a little. "I wish I didn't have to, but you heard the boss lady."

"I know," I answer, defeated.

He gets up from the bed and gets dressed. I grab the robe from the floor, put it on, and we walk down the stairs. Each step I take is in slow motion. My mind is racing with all the things I want so desperately to say to him. I want to tell him how I feel about him. I want to tell him who I really am and how I wish to renounce my angelic status so I can be with him, but the words don't come.

"I'll probably end up coming in late to school tomorrow," he says as we stand by the front door.

"Yeah, I figured as much."

He pulls me toward him and wraps his arms around me. He is a few inches taller than I am, and my head rests perfectly and comfortably at his neck, right underneath his chin. I breathe him in, savoring the scent of sweat-tinged cologne. I want to bottle that fragrance, keep it forever, and wash my soul with it. "See ya tomorrow?" he asks.

I nod my head, but the tears come over me again.

He lifts my chin up so we are looking each other in the eyes. "You're not allowed to do that," he says. "My angel is not allowed to cry." And he bends down and kisses me. My insides spin dreamily at the touch. His deep kiss washes away all my negative thoughts and feelings. When we stop, he looks at me again, smiles, and kisses my forehead.

The highest Level of Humanity is Enlightenment. I had always assumed that when an angel completes and succeeds in the mission, they would reach the ultimate level of Enlightenment—a state so holy, that they would be granted their return to Ilarium. And as I look into Jake's eyes, grip his hand tighter, let the feeling of his kiss linger throughout my very soul, I am convinced I have found my true Enlightenment.

As he leaves, my heart shatters onto the floor. Hopelessness nearly rocks my body into uncontrollable sobs, but I never get that far because Aunt Ruth is waiting for me at the top of the stairs. She drums her fingers on the banister, "Done down there?" she asks.

"Yes," I reply flatly, vacantly, as she comes down the stairs.

"You know what happens next, don't you?" she asks in the same calm tone she used before.

I nod. "Yes. I know. My mission is over, isn't it?"

She touches me on the shoulder. "Yes, Aestra, it is." There's real pain in her voice—pain that's laced with disappointment.

"Did I fail?"

"We don't know. It's going to be considered 'unresolved' until he makes his final decision. So, there is a possibility of failure, but we're not sure yet."

"Okay," I say.

"In the meantime, you need to go back to Ilarium. There, you will be taken in by Camael to wait your judging."

My body stiffens. "Judging?"

"The Dominions are going to review your case. But let's be honest here, you knew this would happen. You knew full well what you were doing and you knew there would be some consequence. You had to have..."

"Yes," I answer. Reviewed. Judged. And I also know that being cast out of Ilarium is also a possibility. "I knew."

Aunt Ruth sighs heavily. She looks old, almost ancient. The lines around her eyes are deep set and her makeup is cracking around it.

"You'll be leaving at once," she says.

"How?" I ask. "How do I get back there?"

She goes into the kitchen and comes back with what looks like a medical vial used to collect blood. Only, there isn't blood in it, there's a purple iridescent liquid within the glass container. She hands it to me. "When you're ready, you're to go to the park where you descended and drink the contents of the ampoule."

When I'm ready? I'm not ready. I won't ever be ready. "When will I be ready?"

"Trust me, you'll know."

"What happens then?" I ask.

"Isn't it beautifully human to question the unknown?" she responds. And that's all she says about it.

"And what about Aestra. Aestra O'Neill? What happens to her?"

She shakes her head. "Ran away during the night. We had an argument, and she took off."

I finger the vial. "Uh-huh. I see," I say and proceed to walk upstairs.

"I'm sorry I failed you, Aestra," she says, her voice trembling, but I ignore her.

I go back to my room and try to get some sleep, but that's an impossibility after all that has happened. I've experienced the most extreme of human emotions in such a short time span that I feel like I'm on overload, overdrive. My inside engines are racing at top speed. I couldn't sleep even if I tried. My mind is scattered, jumbled. I try to hold on to a single concrete thought, but the influx of information melding with emotions is too much to handle. The second a thought comes into my mind, it flies away, replaced by yet another un-graspable idea, notion, feeling, thought, emotion...

There will be nothing left of the human me in Ilarium; nothing left of the human Aestra; nothing tangible or physical to serve as a reminder of my time on Earth. The medallion still sways on the bedpost. I snatch it up and put it back into its sack, and as I do so, I see the poem that Jake wrote for me on my nightstand. "Aestrangel." I unfold the paper and read the sacred words written within. "Aestrangel," I say to no one. "Eh-strain-juhl. A strange angel. Estranged angel. Aestra angel."

Jake.

He knew me. He knew who and what I was without me ever telling him. His perceptions were strong. He called me his angel. He knew... I read the words of the poem over and over, committing them to memory. If there's one thing I need to hold on to from this short life, it's this—this poem, these words, these memories. In contrast to the beautiful words on the paper in front of me, I look at the brown bag on my bed, and realize what's inside that bag is something I need to purge. Soon.

As the first rays of the dawn begin to poke their eager heads above the horizon, I dress in sweats and a t-shirt. I creep down the hallway and gently open Aunt Ruth's door in hopes of saying goodbye. She's sound asleep, her breathing hard and nasally. I blow a kiss in her direction. You didn't fail me. You didn't fail me.

I make my way to where I began—where I fell, wingless, to the ground; where I saw Aunt Ruth blazing in all her Watcher glory; where I first felt the cells of my body deteriorate and the magnitude of my own mortality wash over me in violent pounding waves. The vial in one hand and the brown leather pouch in the other. I anxiously wait for the disposal of both.

And as if on cue, Malek materializes into my view. He looks magnificent strolling toward me in his black leather jacket and black jeans. Fitting for a demon. Because, let's face it, that's what he is. Behind his suave charm and dangerously good looks, he's no more than just that… a demon.

He looks at my clenched fists when he comes closer and shakes his head. "This is it, then," he says.

"It," I answer.

"You knew I'd be here, didn't you?"

"Of course, I did. You're always here, aren't you?"

He smirks at our playful banter. His face is soft and knowing, like he actually cares about me, like he actually thinks of me as a friend.

But we're not friends. In fact, we're the very opposite. Sworn enemies. Adversaries in an ever long struggle of good versus evil. The epic battle. But none of that matters right now. None of that matters as I stand here, tears in my eyes, knowing I'm leaving the greatest life I've ever led, knowing I'm about to give up the best thing that ever happened to me. Malek is here to comfort me at my final moments in this life. Malek is here, holding me, absorbing my tears in his shoulder, stroking my hair and telling me it's okay. Like we're friends.

"You did what you had to do, don't you ever forget that," he says.

"I don't know how I got myself so wrapped up in this mess," I sob into his neck. "It wasn't supposed to be this way."

"Then, how was it supposed to be, if not like this? Come on, don't beat yourself up for the way things happened. You can't control the fact that you fell in love with your calling."

Fell in love?

I hadn't thought of it like that, but the second he says it, it registers. I think of the two hundred angels who fell from heaven because they fell in love with human women. Ruth's ancestors. The fallen ones. I think of Jake and how I look at him, how I feel about him, and for the first time, I understand. I loved humankind so much that that love over-took me in the form of Jake. Jake. The one I love...

I back away from Malek and hold out the leather satchel. "Take it," I say. "You know I can't take anything with me. It's yours again."

He clasps my hand for a moment, takes it from me, and puts it in his jacket pocket. "I know. But it will always be yours. It was made for you. You would take it back with you if you could?"

I don't need to think about that one. Yes. I would take it with me ... as a reminder of all that I've endured, and the connections that I've made. I nod.

"He'll do the right thing, ya know," he says.

My face twists. "Jake? What do you mean?"

He places his hands on my shoulders. "I'll make sure of it. You won't fail. I'll see to it." His hands are cold, freezing.

"At what cost?" I snap. "I don't need anything, especially from you. I think I've gotten myself into enough trouble as it is."

"No cost. Consider it a favor for a friend."

But I know damn well that favors from demons always need to be returned. I don't want to owe him anything. I don't want to be in his dark pocket. "We're not friends, Malek," I say matter-of-factly.

He approaches and embraces me again. I let the coldness of his fabricated body send shivers down my spine. "Trust me, I owe you more than you know." Still in his arms, I crane my head to look at him. His eyes are dark gray storm clouds shifting across the vast horizon of the universe, but behind the clouds, I see stars... thousands of them twinkling in his pupils, shining with wonder and happiness. Happiness for a demon. He pulls me forward. "I owe you, Aestra," he whispers into my ear. "*You* were *my* calling. My very, very successful calling."

I swallow hard in fear, in shame, but a part of me isn't surprised. I don't think anything can truly surprise me at this point in time. He kisses my forehead, the same way Jake did what seems like a lifetime ago, then he holds out both of my arms and smiles at me. "Time to go, Morning Glory."

I sigh, "Yep. I suppose so."

"I'll clean your house for you, you understand?"

I nod, and the tears spring back to my eyes.

"You know where to find me if you need me," he says.

I uncork the cap on the vial and drink it back. My eyes become heavy, and between the heaviness and the tears welled up there, the image of Malek quickly blurs out of focus. He waves his hand at me, waving goodbye, and an uncontrollable surge of sleepiness takes sudden control. I fall to the cold, hard ground feeling the wetness of the dewy grass tickle my arms. The vial falls out of my hand. I tilt my head to the side. In the distance I see a field of purple flowers—curious looking flowers with what looks like a hundred little eyes adorning their petals.

Chapter Seventeen

Return to Ilarium

When I wake up, my head is in a fog. It feels as if there's a large boulder pressing up against my chest, and my eyes are heavy—I can barely open them. A sharp pain radiates down my back, like the pain I felt each morning I woke up in the hospital after my car accident. A part of me expects to open my eyes to the white walls of the hospital room and to feel the crisp sheets of the hospital bed in my hands. But that was a lifetime ago, a distant memory. My ears strain to hear the sounds of Aunt Ruth in the kitchen unloading dishes from the dishwasher or hurriedly fixing breakfast for herself before work. But no sounds come. I turn onto my side, and the weight of my body feels so unnatural, so unfamiliar. Something behind me makes a whooshing sound against the sheets of the bed I am on, so I force my eyes to open wide. Everything is white; the world around me looks white—like I'm waking from a hazy dream.

But this isn't a hospital room or the room I stayed in at Ruth's house, and the faint hum of music in the air alerts me that this is no dream.

This is Ilarium. I somehow made it back.

I reach my arms around me, and yes... my wings have returned. I caress the soft feathers that feel so alien to me right now. I am fully aware of their weight, their heaviness, like a burden to forever be carried around. Yet, as I tilt my head to see them, they are not white as there they were before. They now bear an odd hue of green and blue and yellow and green mixed all together. The color of Revalia's wings. The color of a bruise.

The room I am in is the same as when I left. It's the same apartment complex structure where Revalia and I lived before we were sent to Earth, but I see things now with my angel eyes. Everything is sharp looking. Edges and lines are more in focus, colors are amplified beyond human comprehension, music fills the air even in the strongest of silences. I shut my eyes tightly to try to block out the intensity of it all. I have been human for some time and I know it will take a while before I am fully adjusted to my true state. Yes, I am an angel again. My aura pulsates a soft lavender tone, like sparkles or glitter reflecting the sun's rays, but I still have an aching in my heart, letting me know that a piece of me is human still.

There is music coming from the living room so I get up. A part of me is very eager to be reunited with Revalia! To my dismay, I see Revalia and Lozhure standing by the front door in an angelic embrace. His wings wrap around her entire body, engulfing them in a sea of navy-blue feathers. Her eyes are closed as she lays her head against his chest. She looks at peace, content, happy, human. Is that the expression I made when Jake embraced me? They look so connected to each other, like a couple in love. Lozhure softly pets the back of Revalia's hair. His long fingers lovingly twirl her sea of brown locks, each strand of her hair dances gracefully around each fingertip. They belong together, there's no doubt about it. They are the only angels that I have ever known in my entire existence to be likened to soul mates. We're all soul mates, but for Revalia and Lozhure, their bond is sealed in their humanity. At the heart of it all, they still have grace and goodness. Maybe The Powers That Be allowed them to be mates as part of their salvation. Or as part of their punishment?

Camael had said they would always have each other because they were bonded by their mutual experiences. A twinge of jealousy grips me for a half second because when I made my connection with Jake, I felt that our mutual experiences would be enough to hold us together. I sigh at the thought of Jake, and can burst out in tears thinking that I will never see him again, never hold him again. Revalia looks up and tilts her head in my direction. "You're awake!" she squeals as she detaches from Lozhure.

I nod my head and take a step toward her. She looks up at Lozhure and kisses him on the cheek. "See you later," he says lovingly. "Glad to see you back, Aestra," he calls over Revalia's shoulder to me. I wave goodbye to him.

Revalia closes the door behind him and turns to me, her face beaming with joy. She takes me into her arms. "Oh, Aestra!" she gushes. "You're home!" But there's a hint of foreboding in her tone.

"Yes," I say, unenthusiastically. "I'm home."

The worry on her face can no longer be hidden. I get a sense that she knows exactly what happened to me and what is about to happen to me. She forces a small smile. "I'm glad you're here."

"I see you're back as well," I say, trying to switch the topic from me to her.

She guides me to sit next to her on the couch. "Yes," she says quickly. "It was a fairly easy mission. I guess Camael chose a more stress-free one for me to boost up my confidence or something. It was a pretty simple one, and it was over fast."

"And Lozhure? I'm guessing he was successful, too?"

"Yes. He had the same deal going on. Easy mission. Easy ego-boost."

"Slider class," I mumble under my breath, thinking about Jake.

"Huh?"

I quickly shake my head. "No, nothing, continue."

"Cam says I'll be going again pretty soon, and I think he's going to give me more of a challenge this time."

"Going again?" I ask, playing dumb, but I know good and well that Revalia will constantly be on missions.

She lowers her head as her aura flashes a hot pink hue. Embarrassment? Auras don't lie. She might be able to hide it from her face, but her angelic self can't control her wave of emotion. "I can't ever move up, Aestra," she says softly.

Yeah, yeah, I know this story. "Because you failed your first mission," I say.

But she shakes her head, taking me off guard. "It wasn't the failed mission, Aestra. Others before me have failed. Regardless of how rare, it does happen. But that's not why I am forbidden to move up the ranks. I will never be a Guardian, never be a Power, never be a Dominion, and so on and so forth, and I will never have the divine luxury of serving the Lord as a Seraph. It wasn't cause I failed my calling. Courtney had deeper issues than her twelve-year-old mind and body could handle. She was beyond my reach. She was beyond anyone's reach."

"So, what happened?" I ask, intrigued.

Revalia keeps her gaze on the floor. "It's what happened after Courtney took her own life. How I behaved towards the humans. I let the rage of losing her consume me, and I lashed out."

"Saw red."

"Yes," she agrees. "That's the only way to describe it. It was like seeing red, an all-consuming, all-encompassing rage. I let it in. I let it pour all over me. I let it blind me."

"Tainted with humanity." Camael's words play loudly in my head, their meaning becoming clearer than I had first understood.

"Exactly. I let the rage in, and set it free on the group of girls who had been Courtney's torturers." She flips her hair forward, covering her face in horror. "I hurt them, Aestra," she says through strands of hair and sobs. "I hurt them very badly."

I can't help but raise my eyebrows. "What do you mean, badly?"

"There were three of them, and the one girl, the ring-leader, I hurt her the worst. Two with my hands, the one with a knife. She needed to be hospitalized."

"Did you have help?" I ask, the words coming out of my mouth before I have a chance to stop them.

She looks up at me, puzzled. "What do you mean? Help?"

"I mean, were you influenced in any way? Was there another force egging you on? A demonic force?"

She huffs and places her head into her hands. "I wish!" she says, her voice sounding muffled from between her fingers.

"And Lozhure?" I ask.

She looks up at me, deeply, seriously. I can see the humanity teeming in her eyes, and my reflection gleams back at me. I can see my own eyes within hers. And I see, it is in me, too... humanity will stay with us forever.

"And Lozhure?" I repeat after a few moments. "Did he hurt someone, too?"

"Worse, Aestra. Much worse."

Worse. The word resonates in my mind and draws multiple conclusions. That's their bond. They both had a moment of weakness, a moment of unadulterated fury that they both acted upon. I understand that all too much. I understand the emotions overtaking you, I understand the heart-pounding desire and temptation to act.

She places her hands in my lap, smoothing out the white gossamer dress that I now wear. "And what about you?" she asks.

I tilt my head forward. "What about me? C'mon, Lia. You know. As I'm sure everyone else does, too."

"Well, I know that they have not declared yours a success or failure yet. I know that you were brought back to Ilarium abruptly. I know that you're awaiting some formal trial. I know that you committed some kind of," her voice trails off, "*indiscretion.*"

I laugh. "Indiscretion? Is that what they're calling it?"

She shrugs her shoulders. "For lack of a better word, I suppose."

Indiscretion. What a fitting word to suit The Powers That Be's needs. Indiscretion. Like what I did was an entire accident, a complete mistake.

"Aestra, what else are they to say about it? How else do you suggest they 'bill' what transpired between you and the boy?"

I could think of a hundred other ways to explain and describe what happened between Jake and me, indiscretion not being one of them. "You're right. I'll probably be cast out, won't I?"

"Cast out?" she squeals. "What would make you think that?"

I raise my eyebrows again at her.

"You're not the only one among us who has sinned. If I wasn't cast out, if Lozhure wasn't cast out, I'm sure you won't be," she reassures.

She has a good point. Angels who are cast from Ilarium are the ones who have committed the greatest sins against the Lord. I did not sin. I don't believe that my love for Jake is or was in any way sinful.

"What was it like?" she asks, her eyes glowing with mortal curiosity.

I blush. "What do you mean?"

She looks away briefly and clasps her hands together. "You know? I told you they were beautiful. Humans. Didn't I?"

"Yes. Yes you did. They are the most beautiful."

She sighs dreamily. "And the most ugly."

"You mean, ugliest."

She gives my shoulder a slight tap with her fist, like the way Summer playfully swatted Jake in the car the night of Vic's party. "You know what I mean!" It's such a typical, human thing to do, a physical reaction to display camaraderie. "Seriously, though, what was it like? To love a human as a human?"

I think about that for a moment. "It was like nothing else I've ever felt before. It was compartmentalizing the word 'love' in new, yet strange way." My throat starts to get tight, and my body tenses up. I stand up as I try desperately to hold back the onslaught of sobs, but I lose control and weep into my hands. "I'll never see him again," I cry as the realization truly hits me. "I'll never be in his presence, never get to tell him how I feel."

She stands up and embraces me, throwing her arms around my shoulders and stroking the feathers down my back. "Aestra, that's crazy talk," she says gently and calmly into my ear. "You're being so silly."

"I'll be alone," I whisper back. "All alone."

"Stop, stop saying those things! You'll always have me. I'll always be here for you and with you."

"It's not the same. You have Lozhure. You know that feeling with him; I saw it on your faces even before I was sent to Earth. He is your mate. That is entirely different from what you and I have. I want that feeling back in my life."

"Aestra, you need to be patient. It will happen for you," she coaxes.

I sniffle. "What are you talking about?"

"Think about it logically. Your calling. He's so important that he needed to be guided by an angel. Correct?"

"Yeah."

"And, his progeny is going to do wonderful things for the most complex creation of the Lord. Correct?"

"Yeah. What are you...?"

"So, wouldn't it make sense that he would be granted Ishim? No lights out for Jake. If he's so significant to the advancement of humankind, that would be his ultimate reward."

I sniffle one last time and perk my head up. Why hadn't I thought of this before? It makes perfect sense. If Jake is granted entrance to Ilarium as an Ishim, I would be able to see him again. A glimmer of hope stirs within me. Revalia is right... Jake is too important to the grand scheme of things.

I wrap my arms around her and squeeze her as tight as humanly possible, as tight as angelically possible. She begins to laugh and cry out, "My wings! My wings! Be careful, Aestra!"

I release her. "Sorry. Sorry."

"No worries, my love. Just hang tight. Cam will call you for your judgment soon. And really, can it be any worse than what Lozhure and I got? At least we'd all be in the same boat. And then you can ride out the tide. Wait for Jake. 'Cause isn't time all we have now?"

We never knew of time until we were assigned our callings. And after embracing the human experience the ways that we did, time is all we'll ever know. I know I'll have to be very patient. Repeating the poem he wrote for me in my mind, I vow to never forget it. And I know I'll have to accept whatever punishment The Powers dole out to me, and I'll have to do a lot of waiting. But I know I can do it—for Jake. For us.

Chapter Eighteen

Lest Ye Be Judged

The hushed voices of the three Dominions scare me. I've been summoned to the dwelling of Drakonas, another high ranking Dominion, and he, Uriah, and Camael have spent quite some time discussing what is to become of me. They have not let me into their meeting room yet, but it's all just the same as I can hear their voices through the pseudo-walls. Obviously, they are trying to be covert in their conversation; every now and then one of them will raise his voice and the others will hurriedly "shush" him. It's comical, actually, to hear them trying so hard to be discreet, when I'm literally five feet from them and can hear every word they say, hushed or not. The good thing about all this is Camael is so distracted with what's going on, that I finally have some free time for myself without his prying eyes inside my thoughts.

They've been going back and forth, presenting possible outcomes for me and the ultimate possible consequences for

each of their scenarios. At one point earlier, Uriah even suggested intervention from the Seraphs. Drakonas and Camael quickly shut that idea down because dealing with issues like these, no matter how rare they are, is strictly a Dominion job. They seriously do not know what to do with me, and to be quite honest, it makes me a little nervous to know that my superiors are at such a loss.

My heart nearly stops when one of them says, "Banishment." It's Drakonas; I can tell from the booming voice. Camael and Uriah once again "shush" him. It's the first time any one of them has actually spoken the word. They all have been dancing around the subject with every scenario they dream up, but none of them have come right out and said the word. Banishment—To be cast out; to be outside of the glory and grace of our Lord for all of eternity.

"Absolutely not! That's ridiculous!" Camael scoffs.

The room is eerily silent for a moment. "Why?" Uriah finally asks. "What is so unheard of about banishment? It's been done before."

"That was another time, and a different circumstance, Uriah, you know that as well as..."

"But look at what she's done!" Drakonas interrupts, followed by yet another collective "shuuuush."

Camael sighs, "I know. I know. It looks bad."

"Looks?" Uriah chimes in.

"No, it is bad," Camael admits. "But there must be a logical explanation for why she did what she did."

"Logic? You want to talk about logic?" Drakonas says. "Camael, let's not sugarcoat the facts here. She had relations with a human. The last time that happened..."

"That's different, and you know it!"

"How is it different?" Uriah says. "It's not as if it hasn't happened before. Two hundred of our brethren fell because of their lust for human women."

"But they weren't banished," Camael says. "They chose for themselves, and left on their own terms."

"But the fact remains that..."

"No, Uriah, you're wrong. You can't compare what they did to what she did. Yes, she was with a human, but you seem to be forgetting that she was technically a human when it happened. And she was merely acting on her human instincts." Camael defends me, and I am filled with his forgiving love and grace.

Again, there's silence in the room. "So, we're back to square one. If anyone has any other suggestions then..."

"What about what we did for the other two?" Camael suggests.

"What do you mean?" Uriah says.

"Permanent angel status."

He's referring to Revalia and Lozhure, and the thinking is to keep me as an angel just as they are. That would mean I would never move up to Guardian or beyond, and I would always have a calling. The thought scares me, but I think I would be okay with it.

Just as I think I could get used to that idea, Drakonas says "No," rather abruptly. "I don't see how that would work."

"I agree," Uriah says. A pit forms in my stomach; I get a sense that both Drakonas and Uriah see the only solution for me is banishment, and I am grateful that I at least have Camael in my corner.

"Think about it, Camael," Drakonas says slowly. "Each time she would descend to Earth, she would become more and more human. It's no secret that Aestra has a deep affinity

for the human race, and there's nothing wrong with that, but after what..."

"She feels too deeply," Uriah interjects. "She empathizes with them on a higher level than I've ever seen."

"It's bizarre, you have to admit that much, Camael. It's as if she was meant to be human herself. As if she rejects the very nature of her angelic being. As if she doesn't want to be an..."

"How dare you question the Lord's divine design of an angel!" Camael roars.

Uriah and Drakonas mumble something unintelligible before Drakonas says, "No, you're right. I misspoke."

"Who's to say it wouldn't work, though?" Camael pleads. "Look at what has happened to Revalia and Lozhure. Their failed first missions came with consequences, but they have leveled out, accepted their assignments, and were successful the second time around. Now, Revalia is getting prepared for a third time, and Lozhure is assisting me in the teaching aspect until he is matched with a new calling. They are flourishing, growing, learning from their mistakes and becoming better angels for it."

Drakonas clears his throat. There's a rattling sound that booms in the room. "That's wonderful," he says, "but the ramifications of her actions..."

"Ramifications?" Camael snaps. "Lozhure took a human life, and you're going to insist on harsher ramifications for Aestra? By theory alone he should have been banished, but because he was under your watch, Drakonas, his sentence is... is... forgiveness? Should we not award the same mercy on Aestra, whose only crime was falling in love with a human as a human?"

I freeze, and the world seems to freeze around me. Revalia had implied what Lozhure had done, and I think a part of me swept that notion under the proverbial carpet. But now, knowing for sure what Lozhure did as a human makes my misdeeds seem so trivial.

"What befell Lozhure is not the same," Uriah says, coming to Drakonas's defense. "Aestra took part in the flesh in every way humanly possible. Sure, she's not the only one who has been tempted, and she certainly won't be the last. She is, however, the only one among us who gave in to that temptation. Humanity hasn't just tainted her, it has more like, infected her. And let's not mention the other angels. We're forgetting that her contact with the others could ruin them as well. What if she decides to spout off about her time on Earth? What if she implants certain thoughts and feelings into their fledgling minds? The ripple effect could be disastrous."

"More so, think about what it would do to her. Each time she would go to Earth, the experience would split her mind," Drakonas says gently. "She would lose herself. The constant human interaction and her natural proclivities toward the human race would only have dire consequences on her psyche. I don't think she's strong enough to simultaneously bear the weight of humanity and the essence of her angelic nature."

In a way, he's right. Could I handle the constant "back and forth"? Could I mentally cope with getting close to and then having to leave each and every new calling?

"You're right," Camael relents and my insides sink low in my fabricated body.

"Then, with your consent, Camael, it's settled," Uriah says.

"There's no other alternative but to cast her out of Ilarium," Drakonas agrees.

Oh, Camael! If there's one time I actually want you to be inside my thoughts, it's right now! Please, please, please, I beg you. Hear me now. Don't let them send me away. Don't let them banish me for the rest of eternity! I promise. I solemnly swear that I will do anything... anything to save myself from banishment!

"The Observatory," Camael sighs.

"Excuse me?" Drakonas asks.

Yeah, um... excuse me?

"Let's not be hasty in this banishment decision. Let's think of how we can help Aestra. There's so much light and life inside her. I guided her throughout her training. I know her very well. I love her very much. To cast her out over human error is very extreme."

"So, what do you mean by The Observatory?" Uriah cuts in.

"What if we sent her there? To observe. To watch. If she can truly, fully understand humans on every level, and not just the ones she's tapped into, then she could possibly be of use to us."

"Are you suggesting that we confine her to The Observatory?" Drakonas asks.

"Maybe not confine in the strictest definition of the word, per se, but that would be where she would spend the majority of her time. Watching. Observing. Learning. Understanding the extent of her actions."

"I don't know," Uriah hesitates. "I don't see the good that could come from that. Wouldn't you think that Aestra's constant observations of humankind will only drive her mad? If she's that tuned into their nature, wouldn't the divide of her psyche eventually be imminent?"

"Time will only tell for sure," Camael says, standing firm in his theory, "but I think it will be the exact opposite. I think she could use her natural affinity for humankind to her advantage and truly soak in their nuances and quirks and imperfections."

"And in The Observatory, she could eventually impart that knowledge to other angels before they disengage. Almost like a final teaching. An ethics training if you will." I can almost hear the hum of the light of understanding go off in Drakonas's mind. His tone seems to indicate that he's all for Camael's suggestion.

"How not to behave," Camael chimes.

"And if she's good at it, maybe we could allow her to be a liaison to the Watchers. That would then benefit us because it would surely lighten our workload!" Drakonas jokes.

There's movement from within the room, and I envision Uriah, the skeptic, pacing back and forth, his illuminated feet narrowly grazing the misty mirage of a floor beneath him. This decision must be hard for him, as he is the elder of the three and is so very close to transcending to the level of Ophanim. I surmise that the last thing he wants or needs right now is the controversy of banishing an angel. He is taking his time with what is presented to him, digesting it fully before making his decision.

Uriah must have nodded his head or put a loving hand on his shoulder because Camael says, "Thank you," in a humbled tone.

I sigh—a little bit with relief and a little bit with fear. I don't know what the terms of my new assignment will be, but I imagine I will be secluded from the other angels. I'm not sure how I feel about this. On the one hand, I think I might get lonely being constantly secluded, but then again, the prospect of being able to have time for myself, watching the humans, watching Jake, is rather nice.

The three of them move closer to the door. I'm a little surprised that I wasn't invited in to speak on my own behalf, but the more I think about it, the more I realize that was probably a good thing. I was infuriated at the word "banishment," and as I'm trying to shed the last remnants of my human side, I might not have reacted cool and collected.

"Let me ask you this, Camael," Uriah says before the three walk out into the hallway. "What is her strong connection to the human race all about? Where do you think that stems from?"

Good question, Uriah. One that I really haven't given much thought to.

"Yes," adds Drakonas. "It's almost as if she's too much of an angel to handle being human and too much of a human to handle being an angel."

"Whatever it is, you know that she needs to be kept watch over, right Camael?" Uriah says.

I never thought of it the way that Drakonas put it. Too much human for angels, and too much angel for humans? This puzzles me. Are they suggesting that there is something wrong with me? That I'm some sort of aberration? I always felt and always loved... I loved everything and anything because it was filled with the divine essence of the Creator. I think it may be connected to the fact that I so loved the Lord.

"Because she so loves the Lord," Camael responds, alerting me that he's tuned back into my thoughts.

When he walks out, he smiles at me. A weak smile. A not-so-encouraging smile. A smile so feeble that I become almost fearful of what lies ahead. A smile so pathetic and almost fake that I realize the next stage of my journey will not be a simple one.

CHAPTER NINETEEN

THE WINDOW

Camael asked me if I wanted to shed my human shape to which I vehemently refused. It's become a part of me now, so much that I don't think I would feel comfortable not having it. It is me... this is me. I'm sure the same was asked of Revalia and Lozhure, and they, too, must have had the same response. Uriah and Drakonas, and possibly Camael, probably agree that it's part of our "infection" with humanity. That's okay with me. I enjoy my shape. I enjoy every aspect, every curve, every little last detail, because, let's face it, I enjoyed being human.

My angel mind knows things beyond human comprehension, and being here in The Observatory gives me a constant inflow of even more information. It's a pure energy that radiates throughout the walls of the temple. Every angelic deed ever done is here, in this room, like a living, breathing history book. I can adjust my senses to notice certain conversations,

hear certain tales, and feel the strong emotions attached to them. In this temple, I have power. It's a power above and beyond what other angels have, because here, I'm privy to knowledge, and knowledge is the ultimate power.

For the most part, I will be secluded from the others. When others come to The Observatory to disengage, I will be able to interact with them, give them some advice from my studies and a few parting words before they embark on their missions. When they are re-absorbed, I will be here to greet and comfort them. Now that Revalia will be constantly going on missions, I will be able to see her quite frequently, and Camael brings the other angels here on their disengagement day, so I get to see him as well, but outside of that, I am alone. This doesn't entirely disappoint me, because I don't really know how to interact with the others anymore. Besides, I want to wait for Jake.

The light in the center of the room, where the angels disengage, is strong in energy. Too strong. I try to stay away from it in fear that I won't be able to control myself from jumping right into it. Often, I wonder what would happen if I did. Would I end up back on Earth? Would I cease to exist? I dare not ask these questions out loud for I fear I would be punished; however, I think that Camael has left me. I can't feel him poking and prodding on the insides of my angelic mind anymore.

The Window is where I spend most of my time. I soon learn that Lozhure was wrong about the way the power of the Window works. Perhaps it was different for Revalia and him because they were trespassing, and the higher power of the Window limited their line of sight of the world, almost like a defense mechanism. For me, I see everything, not just my calling. All I have to do it think of a place and the Window shows it to me. China? There. Istanbul? There. Brooklyn?

There. Camael told me that my job is to study all walks of human life from every nook and cranny on the globe. Rich, poor, young, old, every race, each sex, the fortunate, the unfortunate, the tragic, the charmed. Study. Study. Study. Observe. And, I've been doing that, for the most part, but I can't help but always bring my attention back to Brooklyn, New York. Back to Jake...

He waits for me at the café in the morning. It's the day of our project presentation, but I know he wants to see me for reasons other than school and some dopey project. He asks the skinny waitress if she's seen me, and she says no. Vic and Summer are at a table close by. Summer shoots Jake dirty looks and whispers into Vic's ear. They laugh together. Jake's face flushes with red anger, but he keeps himself composed and ignores the two of them.

When he gets to school, he waits for me by my locker. Malek approaches him, a pained expression on his face. "She's not coming today," he says to Jake.

"What do you mean?"

"Dude, you have no idea what went down, do you?"

Jake's face twists with irritated curiosity. "Care to explain?"

"That aunt of hers is a real wicked witch! The two of them had some major blowout and Aestra took off."

"Took off? What are you talking about?"

Malek casually leans up against the metal lockers and runs his hands through his hair. "She left. Ran away."

"Oh, yeah? Where'd she go?" Jake asks in disbelief.

Malek shrugs his shoulders. "How should I know?"

"Well, you claim to know a lot, so tell me, how the hell do you know all this? You mean to tell me that she actually came to you before she left?"

Malek nods his head.

"No. Aestra wouldn't leave like that. She wouldn't leave without talking to me first."

Malek huffs and takes out his cellphone. "I can show you the text messages if you don't believe me..."

Jake snatches it from his hands and pushes some buttons. I can't read what's in Malek's inbox, but apparently, by the look on Jake's face, Malek must have glamoured a text message supposedly from me. "No. No way, man," Jake says, shaking his head.

"Look, I know it's kinda hard to believe. I was surprised myself when she met up with me at the park and said she was taking off. I tried to stop her, but..."

"Wait," Jake interrupts. "Were you two...?"

"Oh no!" Malek gasps. "Aestra and I were really good friends. I looked at her like a sister. There was never anything..." Jake hands Malek his phone back. "Here," Malek continues as he takes out a brown leather pouch from his pocket—my brown leather pouch. "She told me to give this to you." He opens the bag and Jake cups his palms together. Malek shakes the bag into Jake's hand, revealing the medallion.

Jake holds up the necklace by the chain and stares at the diamond-shaped medallion. "Her necklace?" Jake asks and Malek nods.

It's my amulet—the one Malek gave me, the one that got me into so much trouble, the one that brought me so much happiness. But it's not mine. The energy from it is gone. There's no more magic swirling around it, no more black ghost fingers to entice and entrance, because that's the part of the necklace that belonged to me. Now the necklace belongs to Jake. I get a closer look at the silver charm, and it, too, is changed. There's an inscription in the center of the metal. It says "Aestrangel" in script writing, and when Jake sees it, he smiles. "Thank you," he says. Malek hands him the brown pouch and Jake puts the necklace securely back in its place.

That afternoon in Creative Writing class, Mrs. P. calls Jake and me up to give our presentation. "Aestra's not here today," he tells her, "but I got this."

Mrs. P. hooks up Jake's laptop to her projector and shuts out the lights. He proceeds to go through each slide of the Power Point presentation, explaining to the class the evolution of poetry over a time period of three decades. At the conclusion of the presentation, he tells everyone that poetry is still evolving today. He clicks to the last slide of the presentation and the "Aestrangel" poem appears on the screen. He reads it to the class and the presentation ends with a deafening applause from the class. We did good.

Jake headed off to NYU that fall and studied anything and everything related to literature. For a while, he searched for me, using the internet to try to locate my whereabouts. He started a message board on a social networking site, but without a picture of me, he basically got nowhere.

He faltered a bit in his second semester when he took a tough writing course—a creative writing course, one that he should have aced easily, but the fire was gone. His creative spark diminished. The poetry was absent from his soul. Summer and Vic contacted him from Europe, and because he was frustrated with school and a little depressed, he almost quit before the semester was over to meet them in Prague. Right before he got a chance to turn in his final withdrawal papers, he met Angela in the main office. Angela was a literature major as well, and she worked part-time in the office as part of her work-study program. Jake was impressed with her dedication, and there was no denying her striking good looks. He tore up his withdrawal form and wrote his phone number on the back of one of the torn pieces. My heart ached at his flirtatious actions, but for me to think that he would remain alone the rest of his life was ridiculous. I knew that Angela was the one he was meant to meet, the one I was meant to lead him to.

Later that night, he used his computer to have what they call "facetime" with Summer. He told her he was staying in school, but would love to meet up with them in Germany the following spring break. Summer yelled and cursed at him, calling him a coward and a horrible friend. Jake closed his computer before she could berate him further. That was the last contact he ever had with her.

I hear voices around me. Camael. Revalia. Other angels preparing to disengage. "Aestra," Camael says gently as he taps me on the shoulder, breaking my stare from the Window, "the others are ready for you. Now is your chance to do your job. Make some good happen."

I turn and see them gathered in a circle around the light source. Their eyes are filled with awe and wonder, and I know that each one of them is anxious to submerge themselves into the pure energy. I walk to each one, lean close to their ear, and whisper softly the best pieces of advice I have to offer. "Don't fall in love. Don't get too close. Don't try too hard. Enjoy your human shell." I dispense my guidance as if I were handing out verbal business cards, and after I leave each of them, I notice their faces are twisted with confusion. They don't understand. How can they?

"I'll see you soon," Revalia says with a sadness in her eyes.

"Good luck," I answer, but it's a half-hearted response. I wish they would all leave so I can go back to the Window. I don't know how many human years will pass in this short amount of angel time, and I truly cannot afford to miss a thing from Jake's life.

Camael sighs. The disappointment is written all over his face.

When they are finally gone from my place, I return my attentions to the Window. I see that Jake and Angela have grown close, and while no relationship comes without its problems, they are able to weather their numerous storms and marry after college graduation. I delight in seeing their arguments because whenever they have an issue, Jake goes somewhere alone and thoughtfully clasps the brown leather pouch. He never told Angela about me, but he thinks of me often, and it pleases me to know that I am still in his heart.

On his wedding day, he held onto the necklace nervously as his future bride walked down the aisle of the church. Despite the fact that he genuinely loved Angela, I can't help but think that he wished it was me walking towards him to become Mrs. Jake Parker.

The years go by in a blur. Jake became a high school English teacher and they moved to California. There, they had two children—first a boy, Daniel, and then a girl, Aestrid. The location, the daughter's name... all references to me. Like, he was still searching for me, still pining over me, still loving me. When his curious little ones asked him about what he was like as a kid, he told them stories about their grand-mother who passed away, about what it was like growing up in Brooklyn, and about the strange angel he met in high school who helped him through a tough decision. Me. "If it wasn't for her," he would say, "I would have never met your mom, and the two of you wouldn't be here today!"

Unfortunately, tragedy struck the family when, at the age of eleven, Aestrid was in a fatal school bus accident. Jake broke down many times, and even "spoke" out to me, wishing I was there to help him through that horrific time in his life. He turned away from his wife, the death of their child driving an unspoken wedge between them. Before Aestrid was buried, Jake tucked the original copy of the poem "Aestrangel" into her hands. Kissing her on her cold forehead, he told Aestrid that the strange angel he named her after will always be with her now. He contemplated giving her the necklace but stopped himself at the last moment. He couldn't part with it.

He couldn't part with me.

Daniel grew up to be a good, hard-working man, but he was not a brilliant human being. He married his high school sweetheart, found a job in construction, and had three children of his own. I didn't see the connection at first to the importance of "Jake's progeny", because at first glance, it didn't seem that Daniel, or even Daniel's children would aspire to greatness. Just when I was starting to believe that I was tricked, duped, Jake retired from his teaching position after forty years of dedicated service. His boss threw him a lavish retirement party, and that's when I saw the real fruits of his labor. His students. His progeny. Wave after wave of former students surrounded him, regaled him with memories, profusely thanked him for his love and guidance and wisdom. "I became an engineer; thank you for teaching me how to read fluently." "I became a pediatrician; thank you for always encouraging me." "I'm a published author; thank you for helping me write an essay." "I'm a nuclear physicist; thank you for helping me with the bullies in 9th grade." Comment after comment. Compliment after compliment. Every one of them loved Mr. Parker. He helped them, educationally and socially. He helped to form them into great men and women. His progeny is of great importance to the entire human race. His descendants will be instrumental to the lives of millions upon millions of people. In forty years, he taught thousands of students who have done just that... been instrumental to the grand scheme of human existence.

I scarcely notice when Camael or Uriah come to The Observatory with angels anymore. Neither of them asks me to impart my knowledge onto the new ones either. Perhaps they have given up on me? Does it even matter at this point? The years continue to race by in a blur, and I am entranced...

After fifty-plus years of a marriage, and at seventy-five years of age, Jake and Angela moved back to Brooklyn. With his father and step-mother long gone and buried, he decided to no longer rent out their brownstone, and he and Angela settled there, hoping to enjoy the last years of their lives in happiness. Plagued with the death of their daughter, it was no secret that Jake and Angela didn't have the greatest of marriages, but they did love each other and wouldn't have stayed together if they didn't truly want it to work out.

Daniel's three sons were married with children of their own. Jake's youngest grandson, Peter, had always been close to him. While Peter's brothers, Simon and Calvin, followed in Daniel's construction footsteps, Peter wished to be like his Grandpa Jake and pursued a career in teaching. Peter moved to Brooklyn with his pregnant wife and enrolled in NYU. When his daughter was born, Great-Grandpa Jake entertained her with the stories of the strange angel from high school, just as he did with his children and grandchildren, only in his old age, he had to fill in some of the missing pieces his human mind had forgotten, and he often repeated himself much to his grandson and wife's chagrin.

Overall, Jake lived a good and fulfilled life—a life that I have watched grow and expand and mature. I am so proud of the man that he became, and I am even happier at the fact that in all his life, he has never once forgotten me. I was with him when he got married, I was with him when his children and grandchildren and great-grandchildren were born, and I was with him when he went through the untimely loss of his daughter. I was with him throughout all of his accomplishments, and I was even with him when he held his wife against him at night. The memory of me, the thought of me, the dream of me, haunted him throughout his life. And I've waited here for him, too.

Now, he's at the end of his wonderful life. Eighty-eight years old and surrounded by his family. The end is close for him, as cancer has eaten away most of his body. He fought a good fight for the last three years, but he is slipping... the disease is too aggressive despite his fighting efforts. I am with him now. Using both of his feeble hands, he holds on to the necklace as tight as possible. Angela and Peter are at his side. She touches his forehead lovingly and tells him that it's okay to go, that he did a great job and the evidence is in the legacy he's leaving behind. He closes his eyes, and his youngest great-granddaughter breaks into heaving sobs for her Poppa. Angela bends over Jake, unsteady herself in her old age, the pain of her arthritis surging its way throughout her bones. Peter helps to steady his grandmother, and when she catches her balance, she's able to kiss Jake on the cheek before he dies. The room goes cold and silent.

My hands ball into excited fists. While I am saddened that the human side of the Jake I loved is gone forever, I anticipate being reunited with the essence of his soul. I have waited so long.

Chapter Twenty

THE FALLEN

I wonder how long it will be before Jake is granted asylum in Ilarium. I wonder how long I will have to wait before I am able to see him again. I wonder how long I have to wait before I can embrace him in his new form and tell him all the things I have longed to tell him. Revalia and Lozhure have their special connection, and I will have mine. Soon. I have done all that has been asked of me. I have accepted my punishment. I have made my repentance. I have fulfilled my angelic destiny, and now, I wish to live for all of eternity with the soul I am so deeply connected with.

The room suddenly goes dark. The Window had revealed to me the last moments of Jake's life flickers to a black screen. I reach my hand to touch its velvety surface, and there's no longer a sense of pulsating life therein—just an empty canvas. A shiver runs through my body and when I turn my head to look at the light source in the middle of the room,

I see that it, too, has been diminished. The room gets very cold, very fast.

"Hello?" I say. How stupid of me? I know there's only me here. I'm alone and have been for the most part, for a very long time, but this sudden eerie change of scenery is enough to spook me.

My voice echoes off the tower, sounding alien to my own ears. Has it been that long since I've actually used my voice to speak? I start for the door, hoping maybe there is someone else in another section of the temple who could explain to me what's going on, but my feet won't budge. I can't move. I'm frozen in place. I attempt to use my angelic instincts and try floating to the door, but that's of no use, either. I'm stuck.

No. I'm not stuck. I am floating, but it's beyond my control. I'm being lifted into the air by an unseen force, being pulled upward by an invisible rope strapped around my waist. The walls of the room are melting, dripping away like water on a painting. This must be it! This must be how I will be reunited with Jake. I am going to meet him for his ascension.

The Lord has heard my prayer.

The temple melts away completely and I am left suspended in midair. Darkness and silence engulf me. There's an odd sensation of absence. Nothingness. Emptiness.

I'm suddenly afraid.

"Be not afraid, Aestra," a voice booms in my mind. It speaks to me not with the human languages I have been so accustomed to, but with the language of my kin, the angelic words that I have not used for many and many a year. The voice is loud and all-encompassing. I don't just hear it in my head and in my ears, I hear it in my arms and feet and wings. It courses throughout the entire shape of my body, touches every hair and fiber, resonates in every quill of my feathers.

The Creator.

The thought of being in the presence of the Almighty fills me with great happiness. My eyes struggle in the darkness to see Him, to catch a glimpse of His divine essence. But I am met with nothing. Empty. Dark. "Where are you, Lord?" I speak aloud.

"I am here, child," He says.

He's not, though. There's no sign of Him except His powerful, booming voice. I start to panic and struggle harder to see Him in through the darkness. "I can't see you, Father!" I cry.

"Close your eyes."

I follow His instructions and shut my eyes. Within seconds a glorious glowing light fills the space in which I am suspended. The wonderful heat from it warms the very essence of my soul, and pure love encapsulates me. The warmth seeps into the fibers of my feathers, and with my mind's eye, I can actually feel and see the color of them—pink to purple to blue to green to yellow to orange to gold! Golden feathers infused with pure love. "Oh, my Lord!" I gasp as I am lifted higher so. My body slowly spins, dances, moves upwards still into a cone of light and love. I am Dorothy in the tornado, except I'm not in the presence of a wicked old witch. I am in the ultimate presence of God.

The rotation stops, and I am completely weightless. I dare not open my eyes, but I suspect that I am returned to my former self—stripped of my human shape, before the eyes of the Creator in my original design.

"What do you feel?" He asks.

"Love. Light. Life," I answer.

"Why do you feel this way?"

The feeling is overwhelming. The light punctures me at my very core, and I can't help but smile and swoon at the pinnacle of his presence. "Because You are before me, my Lord.

You are the source of everything that is good and sacred in this universe. You have blessed me."

"Yes, Aestra, you are blessed. But there is more to you than what you feel, but you have done nothing but feel for quite some time."

"I... I don't understand."

"And that is the problem, my child. Your power to reason has escaped you, overtaken by the power of emotion. You are losing yourself to yourself."

His light blinks out for a fraction of a second, and for that split fraction, I am frightened.

"Father!" I cry. "Have I done something wrong?"

"You are entitled to choose whichever path you deem fit for yourself. That has always been the way."

"But have I been wrong?" I ask again, unsure now of where this meeting is heading.

"No, Aestra. You haven't been entirely wrong. But you haven't been entirely right, either."

Sadness sweeps over me. I have disappointed the Creator, something that I have never even imagined possible. I wish to weep, I wish to sob, but as I suspected, I am no longer in my human form. My angelic nature has never known of this sadness that burns inside of me, and has no natural mechanism for dealing with sadness such as this. Pure forms shed no tears.

Uncontrollable heat emits from my wingtips. "Easy, child," He coaxes. "For all of your misdoings, you are still my perfect creation, and I am all forgiving if you truly have sorrow in your heart. I could never deny you a place in my realm if you are with repentance."

A burst of energy passes through me, calming my growing sorrow. "Father," I say, "I will do anything to make this right again. I will do anything to be worthy in Your eyes once more.

Grant me the chance to prove myself to You and to the others that I have turned against." With my eyes still closed, I can see the light around me dimming to a soft candle-like glow.

"Tell me," He says softly, "what do you want?" This time, His voice is only in my ear, as if He's standing right beside me, caressing my shoulder, nuzzling my face with his wondrous essence.

"I want to be forgiven," I reply immediately.

"No," He answers. "What do you really want? Right now. What is it that you desire?"

A wet, tingling sensation rushes through me, like water from a waterfall covering my body. For a moment, I dive into that waterfall, thinking about the true answer to his question. What do I want? What do I seek? What do I desire more than anything in this entire span of existence? He must already know the answer, because I feel Him probing my essence in a way that only the heavenly Creator could. Confidently, I answer, "Jake."

His light flickers again before returning to its full brightness.

"I want for Jake to be granted entrance into Ilarium."

"Tell me," He says, His voice booming again throughout my body, "what have you learned from all of this?"

"Learned, Father?"

"Yes. You desire forgiveness, you desire an Ishim, but what have you learned from your experiences?"

I sigh. I hadn't given much thought to what I have walked away with all these years. I've watched plenty of humans and interacted with many angels. I've given advice for them to use in their missions. I've come to understand the nature of the human soul and the power of love and friendship. I've learned to make and keep the very necessities in human life—relationships on levels of basic, acquaintance, sympathetic, empathetic. I've learned self-confidence and...

"Nothing," He says, interrupting my thoughts. "You've learned absolutely nothing."

"Father?" I ask. "But I..."

"Aestra, all your surface realizations have been human in nature. You have learned nothing on an angelic level. Your inability to make the next level connections has been what is holding you back. Child, you have squandered your time spent in The Observatory."

My eyes close tighter, but they're not really eyes, more like openings in a non-corporeal structure. A heat wave flashes against my wings, but they're not really wings, more like slants and slats, cutouts in a paper doll. That's when I realize, my angelic shape is shifting, changing, transforming... melting. I'm no longer in control "No! I didn't!" I wail.

"What value did you serve for the others? What meaning did you give to their assignments? How did you help enhance their success? What did you learn from your observations of mankind?" He questions me in rapid-fire fashion and the light and darkness behind my closed eyes dances wildly. My form is deflating into nothingness. I'm sucked away into a lonely abyss. The love and presence of the Creator being pulled farther and farther away.

"I learned to love!" I scream, my hands trying to grasp at something tangible to hold on to before I am suctioned into a black vortex for all eternity.

"And now," He continues, "as you stand before Me, in the presence of your heavenly Father, your audacity continues to blind you to the truth."

Everything stops and becomes still. The feeling of damnation is lifted and my essence is molded back into my human shape. I'm Aestra again! I rotate my shoulders fluffing out my wings to full span. "What truth is that?" I ask.

"Jake is gone. He is dead. He passed. He no longer exists in that world. Or this one. Lights out."

A stabbing pain cuts into my chest. I fight to catch my breath. Heavy tears well in my eyes, and I understand why the Creator shifted me back to this human shape... so I can cry. Pressure builds behind my closed eyelids, and a hard lump closes over in my throat as I try so desperately to keep the emotion inside. To weep before the Lord is a sign of weakness, and I'm not sure weakness is the emotion I am feeling right now. I'm mostly feeling confused, and I hate feeling confused.

"I don't understand," I say, my voice croaking with fear against the lump. "He was a good man. He helped so many people—he affected so many lives. He deserves to be..."

"The one life that he affected the most was yours. To have your calling in Ilarium would have serious ramifications for you and the others. Think of the precedent it would set."

"Am I to be an example?"

"Of sorts. Aestra, you still cannot see the big picture here, and that is what is most distressing to me. My child, your consumption with your calling is beyond that of angelic or human comprehension. Your emotions run too deep to be figured out or explained. If he were to be granted Ishim, there would be only pain and suffering on the horizon. I cannot allow that in."

"The infection," I say matter-of-factly. "I'm infected, aren't I?"

"No, my dear."

"Then what becomes of me? Is this my punishment?"

"No," He says. "You will remain in The Observatory, but your viewing of the human world will be restricted."

Restricted? Why would I care now? Jake is gone. Dead. Lights out. Those words still don't make sense to me. I waited so long to be reunited with Jake—the thought of his soul, his spirit, being out there only to return to the heavens was enough for me to get through the every day. But this? He doesn't even exist? There's no more breath of life that bears his imprint? Rage builds inside of me, slowly, methodically. It starts at the bottoms of my soles and works its way to the back of my eyelids; it is overtaking me in a way that I expect I will shortly explode, both literally and metaphorically. Jake gone? Dead? Ceasing to exist? This great man, who I set on the right path to benefit humankind, who deserves to be granted the privilege of a heavenly afterlife, who did everything he could with grace and pride and dignity, who suffered unbearable hardships when he walked the earth, is now gone? Lights out? That can't be! Less deserving souls have been granted Ishim!

This isn't fair. I see red. He was a great man. I see red. He did good for Your cherished people. I see red. He needs to be rewarded. I see red. I love him. I see...

As the rage consumes me, I am no longer in control. I open my closed eyes in a flash of anger and defiance. Before me, I see the face of the Creator and am horrified by the gruesome beauty therein. There are twisted dark shapes of gnarled bodies and sharp human teeth. It shines a light whose color is indescribable... it's a color I have never witnessed in my existence before. The mouth of the light opens wide and swallows the heavens and the earth. There is no shape, just a vast expanse of images and memories and tales of the entire length of timelessness. The beauty overwhelms me into shock. The horror terrifies my eyes closed once again.

What have I done? Immediately, I fall to my knees, cowering in sorrow and fear, and I bow my head in reverence.

Fully expecting the pain and agony of being struck down and cast out, I cry, "Please, Father! Please forgive me."

"Rise, child." His voice booms, echoes. The cold stone underneath my feet is like ice as I stand up. The light of the Lord is gone, replaced with a new one. My senses tell me I'm back in the temple, back in The Observatory.

I open my eyes, and yes, I am back. "Father?" I call out, hoping that I am still in His presence. I know I must dig deep within myself to regain my composure, or else the consequences will be severe. No angel acts the way that I have, and I am lucky that I have been granted another chance at salvation.

A rush of wind blows through my hair. "Yes, you may," he answers, His voice trailing upward and out the Window.

He is gone.

He answered my question before I even had a chance to speak it out loud.

I asked to see Jake one last time.

The Window shows me what I wish to see. Jake's funeral, his family honoring him, his friends and former students paying tribute to a man who changed all of their lives. There are many tears, and there are many laughs for the days of old. I'm there, too, as his great-granddaughter presents her eulogy. She recalls the stories her great-granddad told her about his strange angel. The other great-grandchildren, grandchildren, and son Daniel all laugh for they've all heard the tales. An overweight elderly man wheels up to Jake's casket in his electric wheelchair and touches the body on the shoulder. It's Vic, coming to pay respect to the man who was, at one time, his best friend. The room is filled with the energy of the souls of the living; however, Jake's no longer exists. He is absent from the festivities, robbed of his eternal heavenly reward. I can't help but cry as they lower his casket into the ground, to be absorbed by the earth. Lights out. I stifle the growing anger.

The scene in the Window shifts. Angela, Jake's wife, sits at the kitchen table with a yellow legal pad in front of her. A dresser drawer is on the chair next to her, and she and her grandson, Peter, are going through some of Jake's things. She's writing down items and putting check marks next to them.

"Do you think Simon would want this watch?" Angela asks him.

"Yes," he answers as she scribbles something on the paper. "What about his cufflinks? Are they real diamonds?"

Angela laughs weakly, "Oh no! Your grandpa would never wear real diamonds! Give them to Kaelyn, she'll have fun dressing up her dolls."

"You sure, Grandma?"

"Yes, yes. Take them."

Peter continues to rummage through the drawer until he comes across the brown leather pouch. My brown pouch. He holds it up for Angela to see. "Grandma, what about this?"

"Give it here," she says holding out her hand. He hands it to her and she pulls out the necklace. The silver glints in the fluorescent kitchen light.

"Who's Aestrangel?" he asks with a puzzled look.

Angela's face darkens and she shrugs her shoulders. "He had this for forever," she says, putting it into her pocket. "I'm keeping it." And she writes down something else on her checklist.

Later that evening, Peter goes back to his own apartment, leaving Angela alone. She sits at the kitchen table for some time tapping her foot against the ceramic tile floor. Then she gets up from her chair, a process that takes much time in her elder years, and hobbles over to the garbage can. She reaches into her pocket, removes the necklace, and drops it into the trash. The clank of medal against the stainless steel can echoes up to the heavens and my heart nearly stops.

She threw me away!

Now, neither Jake nor I exist in the human realm! My last shred of humanity was welded into that necklace, etched with the human letters of eternity, and now I'm nothing there! I, too, cease to exist!

The rage inside of me returns full force, and I am no longer in control. The red veil drips over my eyes, my aura, and rocks my very essence with a helplessness and hopelessness I never thought imaginable. I throw my head to the sky, and as the tears stream down my face, I scream the most bloodcurdling scream I could ever imagine. My insides burn, my wings thrash. I rush to the Window, pull at the corners of the gold ornate frame, and punch my fist as hard as I can into the center screen. I cry, scream, and hurl my body to the ground in a fit of unadulterated agony.

"This can't be!" I wail, my voice bouncing off the stone walls, reverberating in my ears. I'm losing control, losing control, losing...

In a flash, I'm on my feet and I rotate my shoulders forward so my wings are within my side view. With blind fury I tear at my feathers, plucking them at the quills, letting the crunching cacophony thrill me and the sharp pains surge throughout my body.

"I hate you!" I scream at the top of my lungs. The words flow in the angelic and human voices that reside deep inside of me. They harmonize with an eerie song, "I hate you! I hate all of you!"

Because I do.

There is a blackness emanating from my tortured wings, and I know what I am saying. Most of all, *I mean* what I am saying.

They tortured me. They made me feel like a human. They made me think like a human. They made me do their stupid assignment only to punish the most perfect human to ever walk the earth. For what? To test me? To ruin me? To infect me? To erase me? Or rather, let me be erased by a human woman who knows not of my power and glory? With everything left inside of me, I feel it... the rage, the anger, the betrayal.

I hate them.

I hate them all.

I hate You.

The floor beneath me starts to tremble and shake. The thick stones crack open, and a hole forms in the center of the Observatory. Before I realize it, I'm falling.

CHAPTER TWENTY-ONE

ASPHODEL

I am surrounded in blackness as I swirl and descend. A deep humming comes up on all sides of me, filling my ears with a low, almost mechanical sound. It reverberates in my chest, rattles my very soul. The speed at which I descend is undeterminable. Images whir passed me, and I can barely make out if they are actual pictures or if it's pure blackness churning in this sucking vortex. There are no stars, no earth, no heaven... nothing. Unable to determine if I am both blind and deaf, I begin to panic. Is this what I am condemned to endure? Will this rotating emptiness swirling around me be my eternity?

My body crashes down, answering my question. The ground is cold, hard, and from the force of my impact, I'm afraid I have shattered every bone in my body.

Bones?

When my eyes come into full focus, I'm back. On Earth. I know this place from when I disengaged, from when I drank the vial to return to Ilarium. I turn my head from side to side, scanning the terrain that is so familiar to me and see that I am back on Earth, but I'm not. Not really. Something is not right here. There's a scent in the air that screams of burnt flesh, an acrid odor that burns my nostrils each time I inhale. In place of a flawless blue sky, a brown haze permeates the atmosphere making all that was once familiar about this place unfamiliar with an unnatural sheen of grain—like a permanent gloaming.

I caress the ground and flower petals brush against my fingers. No, I can't be on Earth because the flowers that surround me are the flowers from my very first dream many a year ago. I'm in a field of those purple, eye-laden flowers, but it's the park—the park where I landed and was met by Aunt Ruth! The infusion of images rocks me, makes me dazed with confusion. Am I dreaming? Where am I? Am I dead?

Shadows move in the distance, ghostly shapes undulating in the fog, twisting and curveting like wild horses stampeding on an open plain. My mouth drops when I make out a familiar vision in the shadows ... Jake! He's there—smiling at me from beyond the fog, moving his hand, beckoning me to come with him. Quickly, I sit up on my hands, ready to jump up and run to him. Could it really be him? But in a swift, fluid motion, the shadows converge, and Jake is gone, replaced by another shape that has materialized before me. I inhale a sweet orange fragrance as the figure bends down to meet my face.

It is the human shape of my old adversary, my old rival, my old friend... Malek. He is as handsome as ever, with the silver chain and his diamond gem dangling in the center of his neck. His sleek facial features are flawless—the way his skin is taut against his face, ageless; his bones set high on his cheeks like a vision of a Cherokee god; his hair, dark and silky waves curling around at his temples; his eyes a gray maelstrom descending upon a purple flower field. I stare into his eyes and briefly see myself reflected back. He outstretches his hand for me to stand with him. I hoist up and he smiles when I'm fully face to face with him.

"What is this place?" I ask. "Where am I?"

He lowers his shoulders with mock defeat. "No 'hello'? No 'how are you, old friend'?" he says with a semi-whiney tone. "You know, it has been quite some time since our paths last crossed, and I never got the chance to properly thank you for..."

"Is this Hell?" I interrupt.

"Ah, but what is Hell, really? Hell is just a word formulated by those annoying humans. And that word has gotten such a bad reputation over the centuries, has it not? Fire. Brimstone. Eternal damnation. I don't see any of that here, do you? No, those people with their silliness and fear. People in positions of power needed a way to control the masses from early on, so they created their own vision of Hell. It worked in the beginning, for the most part, but over time, it gave us a negative connotation."

"Us?"

"Mmhmm. Us. The angels."

I frown at him. "You're no angel," I snap.

He smirks at me. "That's what you may think. And, if I recall, you're no longer one, either."

I put my face in my hands, feeling the skin, pressing on the bones, thumbing my earlobes. Flesh. Whole. Human. But not. "So, where am I?" I say, muffled, through the webs of my fingers. "Answer me that much."

"We're where you want to be. This is where you want to be, correct?"

No. Not quite. I wish to be in the brownstone. In my old, human bedroom, embraced by the one I desire...

The field we stand in rotates around us; the mist grows thick and shifts my vision. I hear that rumbling hum again, and before I know it, I'm there... the room, the bed, the dresser, everything is the way I remember, except the brown haze is still present, and I know I'm here but not really. Jake's image is here, too, sitting on my bed, smiling at me. My stomach rushes to my throat in excitement, and I make a quick movement toward the bed, but as before, he vanishes into thin, grainy air. I touch the blankets, fluff the pillows, bounce the mattress up and down searching for some sign, some remnant, some indication that he was in fact there and that I wasn't imagining him. "Jake," I say.

"Huh?" Malek questions, but he must notice the longing on my face because he says, "Oh, you thought you saw him, didn't you?"

"Yeah," I stammer, bewildered, "I thought I saw... but he was right... you can stop with the tricks, Malek," I bark at him. "What is this place?""

Malek sits on the bed and pats an empty spot next to him, motioning for me to join him. "This is Asphodel, the place of endless dreams. Of endless desires and fantasies," he says as I sit close to him. "Whatever is in your heart, whatever you want to see or experience is directly at your disposal. Think it, and you can be there. Does that sound so menacing to you? Does that sound like the Hell they all speak of?"

Of course, the places I wish to see could be accessible to me, but what about the people? I couldn't care less about the sights and more about the company. I say nothing for a few moments, when Malek breaks the silence. "I can't read your mind here, Aestra. The Master doesn't allow us to be so intrusive. I mean, what kind of righteous and just father lets..." His voice trails and he places a hand on my leg, "Oh, sorry."

"Jake's not really here, is he?" I say, knowing full well the answer, trying hard to hold back the rage that is again flaring uncontrollably in my heart. I look at him, and he has a pained expression on his face as he shakes his head, but I suspect that's part of his game.

"Asphodel," I repeat, letting the word sink in.

"Asphodel," he echoes. "And what a wonderful place it is! There's no pain or suffering here. Here, your dreams can come true. You are free to come and go as you please. You're not confined like you were in that space you call Ilarium. Heaven. Hmph," he snorts. "What is Heaven, anyway? Just another word, right? Just another human creation to describe ultimate happiness. But, they got it all wrong, Aestra. The concept of Heaven and Hell is so skewered in the human mind, that if they knew the real truth, their tiny little insect brains couldn't handle it."

"And what is the truth?" I ask.

"The one they praise so heartily, so proudly, so fervently is a puppet-master, and they are the puppets. If they only knew that they were god's play toys, how do you think they would feel?"

I answer without hesitation, "They would probably rebel. Probably renounce their faith."

"Sounds awfully familiar," he says with a sneer. "You opened your heart to the truth, and when you realized you were another one of his puppets..."

"I rebelled. I renounced my faith."

"But here, in Asphodel, that is not the way. Weren't you, the angels, supposed to be his holy children, the ones he doted on and loved so much? And he abandoned you, Aestra. Your father denied your requests, slammed his almighty door in your face, and left you in a tower only to rub in your face the one thing that you wanted more than anything in the world. The way I see it, he renounced you! He abandoned you!"

Tears spring to my eyes, but they are not the product of any notion of sadness within me. These tears are the children of my anger and hatred and despair. I was abandoned. I was forsaken. I was cast out. I have nothing left to give, and I am alone. In an act of sympathy, Malek puts his arm around my shoulder and pulls me closer to him; my head nestled in his chest, my temple grazing the sharp-cut edges of his diamond gem. I pick my head up and train my eyes on the crystalline object. There are hints of muted reds and blues and greens from within the jewel, colors refracting the fog-light in the room. I pull back from his embrace and wrap my arm around his neck, looping the chain over his head.

He says nothing as the mirage of his human shape quickly flickers in and out of existence before his true demon form rises tall beside me. I remember the flash I saw when he first revealed himself to me, but this... this is something else. Black flames dance around his gnarled horns, and his hooves are like iron weights, metallic, heavy, hot steel. His body is twisted and emits a foul smelling stench of rotted flowers and dead insects. I am in awe of his monstrous glory, and I am fully aware of one thing...

I should be afraid.

But I'm not.

In fact, it's quite the opposite. In fact, this vision, this demon, this abomination before me is quite familiar, like I've seen this shape before. I've seen this twisted façade before. I've seen this horrid countenance that split second when I looked upon the face of the Creator. Shockingly, the two bear a striking resemblance, and maybe that's a part of my fearlessness in the presence of evil ... because there is no line between it and the good.

The beast opens its hand, the dark brown and black scales of each claw clanks as they individually roll out like a set of rolled-out knives, and I place the chain within its grasp. The image of the demon sucks back into the shape of a man with destructive gray eyes and a devilish smile. "He wants to talk to you, you know. He has a spot reserved for you and everything. All of this can be yours if you like."

He speaks of the Morning Star. Lucifer.

"Could it hurt to speak to him? Go to him, hear him out, see what he has to say."

"And what if I refuse him? What happens to me then?" Because nothing with Lucifer comes without a price.

"Nothing. No punishment. No reward. He would fully respect your decision."

I frown at his response. I don't fully believe him, nor do I trust him. "So, I would stay here?" I ask.

Malek stands. "In this brownstone, yes, if you wanted. And if you wanted to be on the beaches of California, you could. Or the outer rings of the farthest planet in the cosmos, you could."

"But I'd still be *here*. In Asphodel," I reinforce.

"Well, yeah. Technically."

Because I'm no longer an angel, no longer a human. I am just an essence trapped here in this foggy limbo world, and I fear that the loneliness, and anger, and hatred would eventually consume me. "I basically have no other choice then."

"Aestra, you always have a choice. It's just a matter of whether or not you make the right ones."

I breathe deeply. My chest heaves. I rise from the bed. I made up my mind. "Take me to him," I relent.

"As you wish."

And with that, the room rotates again, and the fog thickens, clouding my vision. I end up in a room made of gray stone. I can see my breath in short smoky puffs, but my body doesn't register any coldness. Malek is no longer by my side, and in his place, the Dark Lord stands. I am now in the presence of the unholy one.

The room is filled with the scent of flowers—fields and fields of different species unknown to both the human and non-human worlds. He, too, is strikingly handsome. Ageless. Pale skin with dark features. His eyes are like two black marbles set against a white canvas; there are no distinct pupils, just blackness, and I cannot see my reflection in them. He wears a long black robe, and the aura that flickers along the outline of his stately posture pulsates the most curious shades of blacks and grays—the colors of death and despair and depression and reckless abandon; the fragments of black lightning from when he fell from Ilarium. His aura is hypnotic; I am drawn to him, sucked into the magnetic space that dances around him like a child's carousel ride. I wish to ride, too! His every movement—a flick of his hand or twitch of his smile—exudes chaos... pure turmoil, unadulterated vanity, and arrogance. In his beauty, he reminds me of the human drawings of the Greek god Hades.

He places his hands folded together in front of his waist. "Because as a human, that's how you were taught to see me, and that's how you see me now. It's a comforting vision, not so frightening," he says. I notice he wears a bracelet on his left wrist—a black leather cord with diamonds held together by silver-clawed prongs. He's hiding his true form from me.

"You can read my thoughts?" I ask.

"I try not to," he says. "I try not to violate the personal space of those in my company, but you are too fascinating, I couldn't control myself." He circles around me, twirling the ends of my hair with his long fingers, bringing the strands to his nose, inhaling my scent. His touch sends electrical waves throughout me. "Do you know how long it has been since an angel has been cast out?" He coos, impressed.

I shake my head.

"An awfully long time. Surely, the others came to me because they wanted to. They renounced their faith in their God, but you... you were willing to stay there in Ilarium. Willing to stay there with your anger and pain for all eternity, confined to that empty box. I find that to be very curious."

I don't know what to say to him. He speaks to me in the language of my former kin as he dances around me and continues to breathe in my spirit.

"I have watched your suffering for a long time, Aestra. Since the beginning of your existence. And I want you to know that I can help you."

"How can you help me?" I say with the language of the humans.

"I can make it all go away. The memories, the pain, the longing, the desire. I can make it disappear."

"Can you bring him back?" I ask.

He puts his hands on my shoulders and looks me in the eyes. "No," he answers matter of factly. "That is something I cannot do. They decided to snuff out his light, Aestra. I have no control over that, unfortunately. That decision is up to them, and once it is made it cannot be undone."

"So, how was it that I saw him here in Asphodel?"

"Because there are still remnants of his being in the world. His child, grandchildren, great-grandchildren, and so on.

A part of him still lives in them, and therefore, there will always be fragments of his soul."

"Then, it's possible for me to will him back to me?" It seems so simple, so easy.

He shakes his head. "It doesn't work that way. He can never fully materialize to you. He will always be like a ghost, haunting you."

I pull away from his grasp. "Then you can't help me." And as I'm about to call out for Malek to come and bring me back to the fog-gloom brownstone, the Morning Star reaches for my hand.

"Wait," he whispers to me, but his mouth never moves. Slowly, he places his hands inches from my face and moves them around my head in a rhythmic motion. There is a sense of pulling and tugging. Is he ripping my face off? "Relax," he whispers again. "Let it all go. It can be like this forever."

I surrender to the motion, let the force field created by the space between my flesh and his cold hands envelope me. It's like I'm being lifted off the ground like my head is being filled with helium, and then it stops. It all stops. I let go, and for a suspended moment, I am free.

A smile spreads across my face, and a warmth creeps into my heart—a warmth that has replaced my longing and suffering. No emotion. Painless. Happy. Free.

When he breaks his trance over me, everything rushes back into place like a rubber band snapping back, snapping me hard in the brain and in the heart. Anger. Blind rage. Disappointment. The shackles and chains of my emotions once again bind me, and I weep. *I will be slave to them forever.*

"Not forever," he says. "You can be free forever. I can make you have that feeling for the rest of your existence. You can be free, Aestra. Free. It could be so easy."

The more he says the word, the more the pain in my chest grows because now that I've had a taste of deliverance, I will long to have it back for all of eternity. Surely, I will go mad. "Nothing is easy," I say with my eyes closed, trying so hard to prevent the tears from falling at his feet.

"That's where you're wrong. I can make it easy."

"How? How can you make this happen?"

"Ah, that is the difference between us and them, dear. You create your own destiny. I provide you with the instructions. The rest is really up to you. You take control over yourself and don't have to rely on the power of others to say when and how you can or cannot do something."

Camael. Uriah. The Creator. All of them. They were the end-all and be-all of everything that I ever did and felt. Nothing got by them. Yes, I had free will, but did I, really? To what end? To be a slave? A puppet? A vehicle for their own devices?

"And what would I have to do?"

"As long as there are remnants of his soul on Earth, you will always be plagued. Haunted. To kill the memories, to kill your pain, to make it all disappear, you must make his soul completely disappear."

"W... what? What are you saying?"

"His bloodline. Erase it. No trace left. Once all the fragments have been destroyed, you will have your freedom."

Kill them? He's suggesting that I wipe out all of Jake's bloodline.

"Kill is such a harsh word," he says. "Eradicate is much better a term. For your end. For your sanity. Because, really, the alternative is your madness. Your soul and heart are too weighed down by the memories, too consumed with the emotions. Do this," he places his hand under my chin and lifts my face to meet his, "and you will have no fear." He leans in and kisses me deeply on the mouth. I am filled with his essence and strangely, his love. It is a feeling that has been absent for so long a time that I barely recognize it at first.

To do this, to commit this act, would be my only salvation. There is no other way for me, for I am so completely tainted, infected. I will no longer long for the human world, the desires of the flesh, the companionship of the boy with the mysterious brown eyes... the prospect is so tempting. For what else can I hope for now, but to be free of him? I can't live with the knowledge that he will never come back, and the soul fragments will surely haunt me for all eternity. I can't endure it.

I am near breathless with anticipation. "Yes," I say when I break from his kiss.

"I promise, the memories will disappear, Aestra."

Aestra.

He says my name, and I cringe with the thoughts of my origins and my journey to the right here and right now. I wish to purge that name. Break the chains of my former slavery. Cut the strings from the puppet master. "Aestrangel," I say. "I'm Aestrangel."

He smiles at me. "Kneel," he commands, and I obey, kneeling before him, closing my eyes, and pressing my lips to his feet. He touches my back and runs his fingers along the outline of my shoulder blades. He's mumbling something that I can barely hear, and I struggle to make out the words, but I know they're not for me to understand.

A searing pain surges in my bones, and I scream from the sudden pulsating energy radiating in my body. The skin on my back is ripped open by some unseen force, warm blood pours down my bent legs, staining the stone floor beneath me. The tendons and muscles and sinews are burning, being pulled at and twisted, fused with outside appendages, and welded back onto my flesh. The smell of burnt skin almost forces me to vomit, but I fight back the bile. A new weight on my shoulders pulls my back into an arch, and I hear a familiar rustling sound.

"Rise," he says.

I obey again, nearly knocked backward by the weight of my new attachment. I can already sense the power within me growing, and that power runs cold in my veins, already dulling the old sensations—love, desire—icing them over in a frosty blanket over my heart, giving me an overwhelming sense of peace and the first sensation of freedom. I rotate my shoulders, and sure enough, my suspicions are confirmed. Strong and pliant wings shoot out and expand at my sides.

He holds out my arms to get a better look at me. "And the world will shudder under her black wings."

But I don't really care about the world right now.

I have a new calling, and I know I will not fail.

Book Club Questions

1. How does the information presented in the prologue shape how you feel about Aestra?
2. Camael plays the role of concerned father for Aestra, but do you think he has knowledge of her "uniqueness" the entire time? Why or why not? If yes, why do you think he allows her to become human?
3. Needs and wants are different things yet can sometimes be considered two sides of the same coin. Discuss the role of Revalia in Aestra's life. What is the connection between the two? Did Aestra need her, want her, or both? And why her?
4. Discuss the relationship between Malek and Aestra. In one respect, she's revolted by him, yet she keeps interacting with him and is curious about his true nature. Why is that?
5. What is Malek's role in Aestra's change? Did he influence her to do the things she did, or did she merely use his presence as a means to justify what was always in her heart?
6. What are your thoughts about free will vs. destiny? How do you feel about Uriah's explanation of how the two concepts are married?
7. When it comes to Lucifer, does Aestra truly have a choice? Why or why not?
8. What is the significance of Aestra declaring herself as "Aestrangel" at the end?

9. Was Aestra justified in her actions? In what ways was she either justified or not when she ultimately renounced God?

10. You've finished the book. Now go back and re-read the prologue in the context of an epilogue. Have your feelings/thoughts/perceptions changed about Aestra (Aestrangel)?

AUTHOR BIO

Maria DeVivo writes horror and dark fantasy for both a YA and adult audience. Each of her series has been an Amazon bestseller and has won multiple awards since 2012. When not writing, she teaches Language Arts and Journalism to middle school students in Florida. A lover of all things dark and demented, the worlds she creates are fantastical and immersive. Get swept away in the lands of elves, zombies, angels, demons, and witches (but not all in the same place). Maria takes great pleasure in warping the comfort factor in her readers' minds—just when you think you've reached a safe space in her stories, she snaps you back into her twisted reality.

MORE BOOKS FROM 4 HORSEMEN PUBLICATIONS

PARANORMAL & URBAN FANTASY

AMANDA FASCIANO
Waking Up Dead
Dead Vessel

BEAU LAKE
The Beast Beside Me
The Beast Within Me
Taming the Beast: Novella
The Beast After Me
Charming the Beast
The Beast Like Me
An Eye for Emeralds
Swimming in Sapphires
Pining for Pearls

CHELSEA BURTON DUNN
By Moonlight
Moon Bound

J.M. PAQUETTE
Call Me Forth
Invite Me In
Keep Me Close

KAIT DISNEY-LEUGERS
Antique Magic
Blood Magic

LYRA R. SAENZ
Prelude
Falsetto in the Woods: Novella
Ragtime Swing
Sonata
Song of the Sea
The Devil's Trill
Bercuese
To Heal a Songbird
Ghost March
Nocturne

MEGAN MACKIE
The Saint of Liars
The Devil's Day
The Finder of the Lucky Devil

PAIGE LAVOIE
I'm in Love with Mothman

ROBERT J. LEWIS
Shadow Guardian and the
Three Bears

VALERIE WILLIS
Cedric: The Demonic Knight
Romasanta: Father of Werewolves
The Oracle: Keeper of the
Gaea's Gate
Artemis: Eye of Gaea
King Incubus: A New Reign

FANTASY

D. LAMBERT
To Walk into the Sands
Rydan
Celebrant
Northlander
Esparan
King
Traitor
His Last Name

DANIELLE ORSINO
Locked Out of Heaven
Thine Eyes of Mercy
From the Ashes
Kingdom Come
Fire, Ice, Acid, & Heart
A Fae is Done

J.M. PAQUETTE
Klauden's Ring
Solyn's Body
The Inbetween
Hannah's Heart

LOU KEMP
The Violins Played Before Junstan
Music Shall Untune the Sky

R.J. YOUNG
Challenges of Tawa

SYDNEY WILDER
Daughter of Serpents

VALERIE WILLIS
Cedric: The Demonic Knight
Romasanta: Father of Werewolves
The Oracle: Keeper of the
Gaea's Gate
Artemis: Eye of Gaea
King Incubus: A New Reign

KYLE SORRELL
Munderworld
Potarium

DISCOVER MORE AT
4HORSEMENPUBLICATIONS.COM